Max Müller

A Creepy
Bedtime Story

SHOOTING STARS

A Shooting Stars Publication
www.shootingstars.co.za
muller@shootingstars.co.za

Illustration and cover design
Brendan Chidrawi
brendanchidrawi@me.com
+27 78 888 1078

Final edit
Sandra Read

ISBN 9781928278108

For Brendan

who makes stories with me

Chapter 1

Born Again

It was a wet evening. It was not raining, but the air was heavier than mist.

I walked along the edge of the curb, stepping on the autumn leaves in the curved water mirrors of the street lights. The houses kept guard on both sides of the quiet little street, hiding behind the flowering crab apple trees that looked rather grey and miserable under the weight of the moisture. A couple of dogs barked far away. As I walked down the hill I could see steam rising from the tarmac, mingling with the aura of the yellow streetlights. I liked it this way; cold, quiet, misty and mysterious here at the edge of the forest, far away from the city.

The bar was toward the end of the road, recessed to make space for a few cars and pickup trucks. Above the entrance was a florescent sign that welcomed me to the Spit and Polish. The entrance lead straight to a long wooden bar counter, heavily bull-nosed above the four legged pine bar stools. Years of wiping gave the pine a grey colour that was neither appetising nor pleasing. Behind the bar was an upright display of Jägermeister on a few glass shelves in front of a mirror, brightly lit to make the bottles seem to float.

A woman, with breasts too large for her low cut t-shirt battled to make eye contact with me. "Would you like something to drink?" she asked. "A Castle Lite Lime, please." The bottle hissed momentarily as she removed the cap.

Bottle in hand, I walked towards the far end of the room. A few candles illuminated the interior which was constructed of heavy beams and excessive wood finishes. It made sense, this was forest country. A few locals gathered around a metal angular fireplace that looked like Darth Vader. They laughed at a joke which I missed and then talked about a young man that went missing after a wedding the previous night. I could see the concern on their faces. "That was messed up," I heard someone say. A man with long blond dreadlocks fed a log to Darth Vader and looked in my direction. "Welcome," he said. I grinned a thank you to him.

I found a table with bench chairs next to the window where I made myself comfortable. I stripped the beanie from my head and shook the jacket off my shoulders, then unscrewed the scarf from my neck. I closed my eyes and stretched. It was an interesting day. When I looked up, the man with the dreadlocks was sitting opposite me.

"Hey. Matthew," he said and held a fist out to me. I reciprocated. He took a sip from his beer.

"Max," I said.

"Good to meet you brother. Where are you from?"

He adjusted his hoodie. The dreads framed his face.

"I'm here for the weekend. Needed to get out of the city."

"I can understand that; I moved here a few years ago and will never go back. It is chilled here. It's a good life." He looked at me as he took a long drink out of his bottle. The fire behind him cast a shadow over his face which buried his facial features in darkness. All I could see were his eyes that followed, even investigated, my every move.

"I envy you. I'm seriously thinking of moving here."

"That's cool brother. If you like, I'll show you round and hook you up with some of my buddies." I could not lay my finger on it, but was fascinated by how unusual his enunciation was. When he spoke, his lips hardly moved and I was almost convinced that he had a lisp.

"I make craft beers in the valley," he said. "This is my brand. Viper. Cool hey? My mate designed the logos and shit. How sick is that?" He turned the bottle so that I could look at the snake label which wrapped around the bottle. The colours of the label, the glass and the contents came together brilliantly. Little holes in the label revealed the beer bubbles and made the scales of the stylised snake shimmer in the candle light. I took the bottle from him. It was cold and a little damp in my hand. I was impressed and cringed at the same time.

"That is awesome!" I said. "Clever to make your product part of your corporate identity. I have never seen that before."

We smiled at one other. "My mate is super talented. I'll give you his number if you ever need work done. Just don't expect a quick job from him. I don't always know where he is because he works on those super motherfucker yachts most of the time. He also had enough of all the shit in the city and found another life for himself on the sea. There aren't taxis and student unrest on the sea - yet. It's a shame because those bastards would make good shark food!" He laughed, turned and signalled the breasts to bring him another beer.

"It's weird that I have to pay for my own beer here, but what can you do?" We both laughed.

I liked him. Alternative is such an old term, but I like 'alternative' people like him. The carbon copy, intellectually sterile human hamsters, GMO engineered for maximum business performance in the city left me stone cold and detached.

"So how did it happen that you moved here?" I asked.

"It's a long story, bro," he said. "I grew up in the city, but always liked the outdoors, so I became a horticulturist. Sitting behind a desk, working on a computer was never my idea of a good time. I liked sticking my hands in the soil, soaking up the sun, making things grow and smelling the different seasons." He turned the beer bottle. The shimmering label cast feint little dots on his face. In the dark his skin looked like leather, motionless. Perhaps from too much sun, I thought.

"So, yeah, that's why I slipped easily into the beer making business. You know that beer consists of only four ingredients: malt, yeast, hops and mostly water. We make malt from barley and a little wheat that grows in the valley. As you know, we have lots of water here in the mountains that taste better than any bottled water you can buy, so it's ideal for a good brew. Would you like a taste?"

"Yes please."

It was only when he pushed the bottle towards me that I noticed the patterns on his hand. Exquisite dark and light grey geometric shapes covered the back of his hand and delicately extended to the first digits of his fingers. I have seen many tattoos, but his was the most astounding body art I had ever seen. The outlines were unlike that of a pen, pencil or even a brush. It was sensuous, distinct yet gentle, like the contours of a pair of lips. Where the skin tone was darker, just a hint of scale-like shapes were visible in the dark, coloured as delicately as the veins on a fresh oak leaf. Once I took the bottle from him, he adjusted his hoodie. I then noticed the matching pattern on his other hand. Strangely enough there were no

11

wrinkles. His hands were smooth as if covered in a thin layer of latex.

I took a sip of his beer. The flavour took me by surprise. It was different from anything I had ever tasted and the bubbles danced on my palate with little explosions of taste.

"You can certainly tell there is a big difference between my beer and that shit you are drinking," he said. "The main difference is that I use decent barley malt as a base with just a little wheat to make the beer a little creamier. The big beer companies use corn and rice instead of barley to make malt because it is cheaper. But cheap malt is crap because it does not have much flavour and that is why the big boys add all sorts of artificial flavourings to make the beer more interesting."

I was captivated. "Many years ago, I backpacked through Eastern Europe and ended up working at a monastery in Lithuania where the monks made beer. They used a very old recipe which they guarded for centuries. I managed to get some of the yeast they used and brought it back with me. One of my buddies is a biochemist and he helped me to grow the yeast. The yeast eats the fermented sugar from the barley and turns it into alcohol. Bubbles are generated as a by-product without which the beer is flat and boring."

"Shit," he said, "I'm sorry if I'm talking too much," and laughed.

"No, not at all. It is very interesting. May I ask you a simple question?"

"Sure, shoot!" he said.

"What are the hops used for?"

"Well, hops give the beer the bitterness to counteract the sweetness of the barley."

He ordered two more bottles of Viper Premium. As I sipped on the beer, his demeanour turned more serious. "There is a secret ingredient which we added that makes all the difference," he said.

"And what is that, or is it too much of a secret?" I asked.

"I'll tell you bro, because I like you and I think I can trust you. I also have a feeling we are going to see a lot more of each other."

By then, the crowd around the fire had left. Our big breasted bartender was wiping glasses behind the counter. It was closing time.

"Let's get out of here," he said. "Come with me."

After having settled the bill, we walked outside. The mist had cleared somewhat and the stars were hanging brightly in the sky. There was not a person in sight. In the crease of the valley, a few cars made their way along the freeway. Their lights made white and red candyfloss balls in the distance. Matthew unlocked his truck, took a

13

six pack off the back seat and indicated that I should follow him. We walked up the hill quietly, past the cottage where I booked in for the weekend, past the houses, shops and park, finally all along a gravel road to the crest of the hill that overlooked the village.

It was a strenuous walk. I was warm from the exercise, but the wind cut through my jacket. My skin felt cold, sweaty and wet all the same. We reached the cemetery at the edge of the forest. A granite bench in remembrance of one of the locals was positioned next to the entrance to the graveyard. We sat down. He opened one of the bottles and handed it to me. Then he opened one for himself. We smoked a cigarette in silence. The mist was thick at the higher altitude which made me feel wrapped in privacy. The moon made a dissipated torch light in the distance.

"This place changed my life," he said.

"How so?"

"I always loved nature. When I lived in the city, I spent many weekends hiking all over the country, but this was always my special place." He looked at me intently. "Once, when I went on a hike in the Drakensberg, a friend and I walked all the way past the Sphynx at Champagne Castle to the crest of the mountain. It was one of the most beautiful sights I had ever seen. On our way back, I was bitten by a snake."

14

"What?!"

"Yes bro, it was hectic. I'm lucky to be here. My friend had me airlifted to a hospital thirty kilometres away and I was on life support for a few days."

"What kind of snake was it?" I asked.

"A berg adder," he said. "Their poison is normally not strong enough to kill an adult, but it affects the way you experience things. I felt as if I was drunk for a week, but it was the most incredible feeling. I started to understand things that were a great mystery to me – I found a different perspective on life."

"Are you being serious?"

"Absolutely," he said, "despite the after effects with which I will have to live with for the rest of my life."

We sat there talking for a long time, drinking and disposing of the bottles in a large drum.

"So when I came here and started brewing my beer, I wondered if I could not use some of that snake venom as an additive to give it a little more kick."

I looked at him in amazement.

"Yes, I saw it as a gift from the Universe and I wanted to share my gift with others. I found a few dudes who worked at the snake research laboratory and we went searching for berg adders at Champagne Castle. We found a few and brought them here. We were lucky because we now have a few breeding pairs that produced a couple of thousand babies for us. We milk their venom once a week and add a drop to every bottle of our Premier range."

I finished the last beer. A small orange halo on the horizon indicated that it was almost dawn.

"So now you know the secret ingredient!" He laughed and looked at me.

When I tried to get up, my legs would not move but my mind went wild. The colours all around us became vivid and animated. The stars made printed circuits in the sky. I was simultaneously in the stratosphere and deep in the ocean. I was amongst fish and birds and furry animals in the friendliest of spaces, but could not feel my body any longer. I was overwhelmed by the unspeakable beauty around us and somehow felt spiritually connected to it. It was a loving space that transcended my previous experiences. I was in heaven.

Then it went black.

I woke up in my room, fully clothed, with a bladder close to bursting. In the brightness of the early morning everything around me seemed opaque and difficult to see. Something was terribly wrong. Panic-stricken I stumbled into the bathroom, turned on the shower, stripped my clothes off and relieved myself in the loo.

My skin felt unbearably itchy and dry. In the shower I cleaned myself thoroughly, then applied a large amount of moisturiser, but the itchiness just got worse. The itch turned into a stinging sensation that felt as if a thousand mosquitoes got hold of me at once. There was a bottle of suntan oil in my cosmetic bag which I frantically opened and poured all over my body, but the oil seemed to be repelled by my skin. Eventually the stinging became so unbearable that I sat down on the shower floor enjoying the little relief brought by the water jet. When the hot water eventually ran out, I felt my way back to bed. My vision became progressively worse – the shapes which I could see earlier, disappeared in a white cloud. Exhausted, I lay down on the sheets without bothering to dry myself. Terror and fear washed over me. I screamed but could not make a sound. Then my body started to convulse, starting with tiny ripples from my forehead all the way to my waist. My back arched as if ancient reflexes that were dormant in me came back to life. Waves of involuntary movements rolled under my skin in vigorous, rhythmic movements that first felt like cramps but then became sensuous as my muscles released themselves of localised knots and spasms. My breathing became deep, deliberate, in pace with the vibration that took control of my body. The reflexive contractions dissipated into a physical frequency that matched that of my breathing. I felt myself floating, lithe, smooth, agile, relaxed, alert and ready.

17

There was no pain when the skin on my forehead burst. There was no blood; just a tear that zipped from the frown between my eyes along the length of my nose. The split in my upper lip brought relief from the pressure in my cheeks and made me yawn. As I leant back, my neck cracked wide open with the sound of tearing paper. I felt relief. The itchiness in my face, neck and shoulders frittered away. Lying on my back I could feel my skin separating from my body - first in little patches, the size of a scab, then it loosened in wider circles until large parts of my body were wrapped in nougat paper skin. As it separated from my body, the convulsions subsided. Finally, the skin on my face became parched and loose in my hands. When I touched my temples, the dead skin covering my eyes gave way. I gently pulled it towards my nose and was surprised by the abundance of light, shapes and images I could see.

My room looked expansive as if I saw it with a fish eyes. The decorations were a little weird. The colours were radiant. I could see a fireplace that looked like the Darth Vader in the Spit and Polish, a large free-standing cupboard and a mannequin over which I could drape my clothes. When the skin all over my body loosened, the itch and convulsions stopped. I stared at the dull sheath that was once my skin. Gingerly, I stood up and removed it from my arms, my torso and then my legs, taking care not to hurt the skin underneath until it lay on the floor like a rice paper sock.

The mirror in my room confirmed that I had a brand new skin, fresh and radiant as that of an adolescent, without the wrinkles that previously revealed my age. I was excited.

It was only when my eyes adjusted to the abundance of light that I saw the faint geometric patterns and miniature scales all over my body; art deco designs that grew in me as if I was tattooed by a master.

Chapter 2

The Village Meeting

It was quite a meeting. Most of the village folk arrived on foot, but a few also arrived in cars, delivery vehicles and pickup trucks. There was a friendly but resigned mood amongst them. Most of the 'attendees' knew each other. Some greeted with handshakes, others with nods, hugs and smiles. One could sense that all was not well. Not quite as bad as one would feel at a funeral; rather more like the concern that one notices at the hospital emergency room after a big accident.

On the veranda of the village hall were two long tables covered in white table cloths. Three towers of saucers were on the side of one of the tables next to a large number of catering cups that were neatly arranged in rows with their handles turned in exactly the same direction. A glass vase filled with wooden ice cream sticks, which could be used as teaspoons, was positioned next to an urn with boiling water. There were three more glass containers, one with brown coffee granules, one with tea bags and one with sugar.

The second table provided space for a stack of paper plates, white No Name Brand serviettes and four elongated aluminium platters with thin ham, cheese and tomato sandwiches, neatly cut into triangles.

Two elderly ladies from the Presbyterian Church, down the road, made sure that everyone received a drink and something to eat before the meeting. When nobody noticed, they hid all the dirty cups and used plates in a large box under the tablecloths.

At exactly seven, a tall emaciated man opened the large creaking double doors and invited everyone in. Electric light poured through the entrance. Inside was a podium with two chairs in front of the stage, which was closed for the moment with heavy red dralon curtains. Large valances with gold fringing garlanded the fraying fabric that looked dusty and dulled by years of sunlight. Two blocks of plywood chairs with steel tubing legs faced the podium. The floors, that once must have been magnificent, evinced scratch marks from countless concerts and indoor sports tournaments over many years. In the corner of the room was a pole with a twisted end used to open the row of windows high against the north wall of the hall. Below the windows were a row of pictures of men in ornate picture frames, probably all dead by now, who held positions of power in the village over the years.

"Welcome everyone," he said.

From what I could see, he was the only one formally dressed for the occasion in a black nondescript suit that was at least two sizes too big for him. His pants were strapped around the base of his stomach with a belt that caused the unfortunate garment to radiate superfluous cloth into unintended pleats down his legs. He wore black brogues shined to perfection despite the obvious cracks in the ageing leather across the bridges of the shoes.

The man took his jacket off and neatly arranged it over the upright chair behind him. Hanging there, it looked like the ribs of a wooden headless creature hiding under the thin lapels of the tired garment. When he turned back to the audience, now silent, it became even more obvious how frail he was. His back was slightly arched, weighed down by a slightly oversized head, on top of which was a slightly out of place black wig. Heavy shadows darkened his sunken eyes that stared at the people in the room.

"For those who do not know me, my name is Jean-Henri Desfourneaux, the proprietor of the Cheerio Chicken Farm, funeral director and mayor of this village." His voice had a monotonous, nasal, singing quality that was stripped of the peaks and valleys on which public speakers rely. The fluency with which he pronounced his name, revealed his French origins.

"We are here to discuss the future of our village. As you know our municipality is in financial distress since the new freeway was built. All the traffic that used to bring visitors here now drive straight past us. We can no longer budget on the traffic fines that formed a significant part of our income ..."

"Never mind the traffic fines," a woman shouted from the back of the room. "Our restaurant is going to the dogs. We have hardly had any visitors coming in for breakfasts or waffles. Two years ago I employed twice as many staff – and I'm going to have to let the remaining ones go too." It was Minnie, the owner of the waffle and deli shop. It became famous amongst locals and visitors for its Belgian waffles which she served with a delicious selection of sweet or savoury fillings.

"Yes, and my pub is struggling as well." It was Paul from the Spit and Polish. "We have had hardly any passing trade for the past few months. Things are getting very tough. If it was not for the regular local clients, especially the guys from Venom Beer, we would have seen our asses a long time ago."

Desfourneaux stood quietly, locked his hands together and rested his chin on the bony finger ball.

An imposing, well dressed woman stood up. She looked as if she visited the hairdressers immediately before the meeting. Her hair was immaculate, light brown with blond streaks, cut in a bob that resembled Hillary Clinton's. It was Fiona, the owner of the little shopping complex at the top end of Main Road. Many people wondered if she wore the clothes in her boutique and then sold them as new because she always looked as if

26

there was still a price tag hidden somewhere on the creations she wore. Few would argue that she personified local style and sophistication. There were even rumours that nobody had ever seen her in curlers. Apparently, when she went to have her hair done, there was a special cubicle where she could be styled in private.

"Friends," she said. "We are all in the same boat. Our clothing sales have plummeted and our occupancy rate at the cottages have hit the lowest level ever. I realise that unless we do something drastic to turn this village around we are all going to suffer. Our old age home and retirement community rely on us to bring sufficient business into our village to maintain a high level of service, but we are just keeping our heads above water. As you know me, I am not one that will easily surrender to a bad situation, so I have come up with a comprehensive plan for the resurrection of our village." Everyone in the room looked at her, stunned.

"The key to our success is that we have to stand together," she said. "We have fantastic infrastructure which we have to use to our mutual advantage."

At that stage she walked to the front of the room, stepped up to the stage, disappeared momentarily behind the curtains and reappeared with a large white cardboard with a mind map drawn on it. The different elements were in colourful circles with interconnecting lines.

"Get us a stand please Jean-Henri," she said to the old man, then turned towards the audience and put her most radiant face on.

"Well," she said, waving a freshly manicured finger in the air, "we cannot afford to live as victims in this village any longer. We have to differentiate ourselves and capitalise on our existing business and know-how. The trick is how we apply that in a new world. The old dreams are dead. These difficult times require a brand new way of thinking."

Desfourneaux, clearly put out by the arrogance of this hair and nail nightmare, coloured in *Mac Rouge Combustion*, positioned the stand next to the podium and secured the map in place for everyone to see.

"Get us a spotlight please Jan-nri," she ordered the old man and then turned back to the audience with a whiter than white smile. Desfourneaux walked to the back of the hall where the sound proof production booth was located.

"Look at me," she said, "I overcame terrible times and a multitude of prolonged adversaries, but succeeded in business and in life. If you do what I say you should do, you are guaranteed success and you will acquire the wealth you deserve."

At that moment Desfourneaux found the switch to one of the two spotlights located on the balcony. The light was adjusted to create a spotlight on the stage, so a large white circle appeared on the red curtains above Fiona's head.

"No, no!" she yelled, "Get the light here, on my plan!"

Desfourneaux struggled up the stairs to the balcony. By the time he reached the spotlight, he was breathless and shaking. Years of chain-smoking, too much brandy and the onset of emphysema left him frail and irritable. He struggled with the light until Fiona and her plan were illuminated.

The village folk looked at her in awe. She was dressed in a pink pant suit with light brown calf leather ankle boots, criss-crossed with dark brown laces. Armed with a hand stitched shoulder bag, by Matewis Maree, also in light brown leather, adorned with a large gold clasp, and tortoiseshell shades, tucked into her hair, she looked like the local winner.

Desfourneaux walked tip-toe back to the front of the hall, making sure not to disturb her and sat down behind the podium.

"Well," she said, "this is my plan. I have thought long and hard about it. Now, if *you* think about it too, you will agree with *me* that we have a few good things going for us. We live in the cutest village in the country. Those thieves from across the border have not discovered us yet, so it is safe and secure here. We have incredible scenery, from the rainforest to the river with all six its waterfalls. The heavens here are unsurpassed at night. Even the old people knew that - that is why they built the first observatory in the country on Mount Pushover, on the other side of the freeway. It is rather unfortunate that the mountain lived up to that name, but what can one say? In those days it was the only place where the locals could get a little frisky around here." She smiled broadly, brushed her eyes over the entire audience and stopped at Desfourneaux.

"Get us an ashtray please Jan-rie," she ordered Desfourneaux, then fumbled in her bag for a pack of Vogue extra length slender cigarettes.

As she flicked her Bic to light the cigarette, an old lady in the front row said: "You are not allowed to smoke in here," but immediately knew that she should never have done that.

"Get it straight grandma," Fiona said, "we need to get this infernal meeting over and done. Either we do it now, or we can all go outside for a smoke and you can balance on your Zimmer frame while we talk about issues of importance. Frankly you need me more than I need you right now. This village can go to shit for all I care and we will see if you can pay your medical aid contributions out of your crappy needlepoint. I have my lion farm for rescues which is going to do well and I will make sure that those cats will recover even if I have to feed them undersized chickens soaked in oestrogen to get them back into shape. Look at this place! I can't spend more time than necessary in this ghastly place! There is more dust in here than the saw mill; it reeks of rat piss and cat shit. So don't be petulant with me dearie - rather prioritise a little weight loss for your osteoporosis. A little smoke will do you less harm than those custard tarts you have in your hand."

Desfourneaux put a clean saucer on the table which she could use an ashtray. She ostentatiously lit her cigarette and offered him a light as well. He quickly took a box out of his pocket and produced a cigarette. "Thank you," he said and sucked on the cigarette, hollowing his cheeks even more. By then, half the audience had cigarettes going. A cloud of smoke started to form in the room.

"Good. Now get us some air in here, uhm, Jannie," she said.

The old man slowly walked to fetch the window stick, hooked the end into one of the window catches and tried to pull it open, but it was rusted shut. Bennie, the cheese farmer, went to help him. They both pulled on the handle with their combined weight. The window creaked, twisted on the swivel hinge and squeaked loudly. The next moment the entire window came flying out of its frame and fell to the ground. The two men narrowly escaped the steel frame when they fell backwards but were cut by the flying glass. The people in the audience jumped out of their chairs (well the ones that could jump) and screamed so loudly that the two ladies from the church, who had cleaned up outside, came running into the hall to see what had happened. The meeting had to be adjourned to get Mary Johnson, who owned the chemist, to rush across the street to get a first aid kit. Needless to say, she was the least qualified to deal with blood. Her experience was more honed in the application of makeup than the cleaning of wounds. She flustered, fussed and finally fainted before Liesie Strydom, a retired matron, came to the rescue from her log cabin. Mary was given a cup of bitter black tea, picked up by two tour guides from the extreme sports grounds and carried to the frail care facility at the retirement village. She was not seen again that evening. Liesie cleaned and wrapped the wounds in a few minutes. Desfourneaux had a nasty cut on his left hand which she covered in a bandage.

"What a bloody mess!" shouted Fiona.

"It is a miracle that the whole fucking roof did not cave in. Jannie, get this mess cleaned! We don't want more people to get cut and I certainly don't want to slip on those glass shards with these shoes with their leather soles." The church ladies felt sorry for him and swept all the glass into a corner. Bennie, who had a cut and a plaster on his forehead helped Desfourneaux to move the broken frame out of the way and made it stand on its side under one of the pictures of the forefathers. Then the meeting could go on.

"Ugh, I have had enough of this." It was Fiona at the podium again. "So let's get to the plan. My recommendation is that we transform this village into a haven of indulgence for lonely people."

"What does that mean?" Troy, a personal trainer, who managed the renovations at Fiona's lion farm and the owner of the extreme sports outfit at the canopy rides, wanted to know.

"Well, it is quite simple. Almost all people feel uncomfortable with their looks and find it difficult to connect with others, even though there are hundreds of social media sites on which people can meet each another. This is especially true when we get a bit older. By fashion standards, we all become awkward and less and less confident. As an alternative, we are going to offer our visitors a get-together experience of a lifetime. They will be able to come here to socialise, drink and eat as much as they like, sleep in beds that are deliciously comfortable, shower in cubicles the size of a kitchen, buy clothes that are stylish and comfortable and experience everything we have to offer in our village and the surrounding area … what do you think?"

"That is madness! Have you lost your mind?" Paul from the Spit and Polish was so upset that he stood up. "Is that the best you could come up with? Why would lonely people want to come here to indulge themselves? There are many places for them to go to."

"Paul, darling," Fiona said, "there are many lonely people out there, but they are paralysed by insecurity. They are being bombarded with images of what you should look like and see the world as a dangerous place because they can potentially suffer rejection and refutation at so many levels. For example, you cannot eat anything from sugar to GMO's. Every sweet thing, with the exception of honey, will give you cancer. If you eat too much of anything you either get sick or you get fat. To add insult to injury, social media have stunted people's ability to socialise and that is why people are lonely and hardly go out. It is a vicious circle. They order take-out food and sit in front of their televisions watching mindless reality series until, one day, they just give up."

Fiona had a sip of water then carried on.

"Since lonely people don't go out or shop, they have lots of extra money which we want them to deposit into our bank account. As you know, I launched our own charge card, called the Indulge Debit Card, which they will be able to use everywhere during their stay with us and at home. But what it means is that we have to position ourselves to get them here before they give up on adventure. We want their money, just like business used to run after the pink money."

"But how are we going to do that?" Liesie wanted to know.

"Oh darling Liesie, let's be ruthlessly honest here. We are all desperate to get laid. Lonely people, in particular, need to get their rocks off. Giving them an opportunity to meet someone and getting laid is enough of a draw card to get them here. There is nothing dangerous about eating, drinking and doing the old horizontal bone dance at the end of the day. We will provide the environment and spoil the living crap out of them without any judgement. We will make all our visitors feel sexy, and desirable and let them have fun – for a price, of course. Now which one of you businessmen have the testicular fortitude to make a serious fucking change to this dying village before all the windows fall out of this dilapidated building with its beastly Plascon beige walls?"

"I say yes." It was Matthew from Venom Beers. "It is time that we upgrade the way we do things here. Almost all of us still rely on all the old recipes our parents had in the eighties, before everybody became obsessed with the things we ate. People became spoilt – they expect the same quality, if not better than they can get in the city. I think we should improve our variety of premium beers, Minnie should doll up her menus with fancy things like 'coulis' and 'canapés', Paul can start using lean mince in his patties, burgers and sausages and Bennie should consider introducing low-fat butter, yoghurt, cheese and milk. We definitely have to market ourselves better by

35

using words like 'organic', 'wheat-free', 'free range' and 'natural'. There is a new world out there and people will not come here if they think of us as an old age home on a hill."

"You are getting the picture Matt!" Fiona said. "But that is only the start. I have many plans up my sleeve.

"Shall we vote?" someone shouted.

Before anybody could even ask the appropriate question, the entire audience put up their hands and shouted their approval.

"Well then," Fiona said, "perhaps the business owners should meet at the Spit and Polish tomorrow night to build a detailed business plan."

After that was agreed, the meeting was adjourned. When all the delegates had left the room, Liesie returned to switch the lights off. Behind the podium was Desfourneaux, hands crossed on his lap, head on his chest, fast asleep. She gently helped him up and guided him through the doors, then watched him walk slowly down the hill and out of sight.

A full moon rose from behind the rain forest. Long shadows crossed the tombstones in the cemetery. A cold breeze blew through the valley, signalling an eerie change in the very foundations of the little village on the hill.

Chapter 3

The Lions

The lions arrived at daybreak on a Thursday morning.

The forest was, as usual, still covered with a thick blanket of mist, as was typical of that time of the day, when the two motorcycles with their flashing yellow lights came over the hill. Fiona was as cheerful as a carnival queen. She had been on her phone to the procession since midnight and was so excited that she almost frothed at the mouth. She paced up and down the hallway of her town house with the parquet flooring and bunches of St Joseph's lilies, tied together with white ribbons in clear cylindrical glass vases, giving instructions to whoever was on the receiving end.

"Be careful, near the entrance to the church grounds, there are road works. Drive carefully. Don't rush, you don't want to stress them out. Did you give them enough water? You don't want them dehydrated when they get here ..."

This was a dream come true for Fiona. She grew up on a farm on the other side of the forest. Her father never wanted to be a farmer, but inherited an exquisite piece of land with views of the valley from an uncle who had neither loved ones nor dependents. Unlike the neighbouring farmers, he decided to grow produce that would be sensitive to the environment and enhance the natural beauty of the land. He planted numerous tea trees along the edge of the rain forest and orange and avocado trees near the farmhouse. During October the orange blossoms smelled so awesome that he eventually built a distillery where he could produce essential oils from the tea trees and the orange blossoms. His oils soon became sought after and produced sufficient income for him to also buy the neighbouring farm, which was as vast and untouched as the African sky. It was a good decision, because the river ran through the farm. There were at least six waterfalls with endless opportunities for adventure sports.

Nobody knew if the old man suspected that there was something wrong with him; within six months after he bought the farm, he was in the grave. His dread disease insurance settled the entire bond and his life insurance policies left a handsome amount of cash in the bank. Fiona and her mother moved into the village and converted three old houses into the little shopping complex on the far end of Main Road, where they sold their oils, fragrances, books and up-market clothing. When the old lady had a stroke, Fiona moved her into the frail care centre of the old age home, appointed a nurse to look after her and went on a trip around the world. By the time she got back, the old lady was already cremated and she finally inherited everything her parents had amassed.

Make no mistake, Fiona knew exactly what she wanted and knew how to get it. Many admired her and loathed her at the same time, but most were downright intimidated by her arrogant self-assurance. While in Colombia, Fiona read in the newspaper about a government crackdown on illegal lion trafficking. She immediately contacted a British charity organisation called Lion Defenders International and offered her lap of land as a sanctuary for the poor lions that were going to be set free. Just to prove that her farm was suitable, she had the property surrounded with electric fencing and built a surgery with recovery paddocks where veterinarians could treat the hapless creatures. Soon after the improvements were built, she acquired two ancient lionesses from the Kruger Park that needed special attention after they were struck down by a botulism toxin – "a naturally occurring toxin that most lions are resistant to" she later explained to a local newspaper reporter, "but sadly these lionesses were old and weak and needed specialist support. That is why I had to do something!"

Behind the apparent altruism and nature conservation was a razor sharp business model. Fiona knew that people would be curious about the wellbeing of these rescued lions and that they would be prepared to pay entrance fees and even contribute to charity funds, which only she was suitably qualified to manage. When the British charity company agreed to consider her farm as a sanctuary for the rescue animals, she had viewing stations installed along the river where visitors could observe the lions. In the final months before the charity representative's arrival, she had a canopy ride installed which allowed visitors to effortlessly glide over the waterfalls and observe the lions from above.

From there she went into overdrive. She appointed an architect to design a new reception building and employed Troy to map out hiking trails, create horse and quad bike rides all along the edge of the orange orchards and to clear the areas next to the waterfalls where visitors will be able to relax in the wild. Troy did an excellent job. He created the visitors' areas at higher ground, so that they can have unencumbered views over the electric fences instead of having to look through the wires. In the end Fiona created her own Jurassic Park, which she called Panthera Park after the genus to which lions belong.

Fiona soon learnt that lions required an enormous amount of food, something she did not even consider when she started with the initiative. She was so blinded by her vision of beautiful soft furry lions roaming around on the farm that she completely forgot to inquire what and how they ate. A week before the two lions from the Kruger Park arrived, she drove to her vet in the city, Harry was his name, and asked if she could feed them pre-packaged food, like the Whiskers she bought at the grocery store or the kibbles on his shelf. After all, her domestic cats flourished on the dry food she regularly acquired from him. Yes, she knew that they were carnivores, but her sanctuary was a place of peace and she definitely did not want to see them killing other creatures for food. Could she have a mixture of fifty 10kg bags of kibbles - from hairball control to bladder support for senior cats? And could she have a bulk discount? In return, she pledged to put up advertisements at the sanctuary for Hills, Whiskers, Royal Canine or whoever, because the suppliers would get enormous mileage out of the exposure. In addition, could she feed them leftovers from the restaurants in the area or perhaps the bones from the butchery?

The thought of death and destruction on her farm gave her such heart palpitations she had to sit down in Harry's reception area, surrounded by bags of dog and cat food for every ailment, age and condition, searching for an Urbanol in her Matewis Maree hand stitched shoulder bag. When Shelley, Harry's receptionist with the squeaky voice, brought her a cup of rooibos tea, she hastily added a few drops of milk and two Stevia pills, then washed the tranquilizer down with a timid slurp.

Dumbfounded, Harry listened to her. It was a welcome reprieve from the normal kitty or doggy examination and vaccinations for the next year. Having grown up in a smaller house amongst the expensive homes in Cyrildene, Harry learnt about the value of a fast buck that could supplement his professional income many years ago, especially now that his two daughters had to get a foreign education after the *#feesmustfall* uprising had created pandemonium at the local universities.

"Fiona," he said, "sure, these foods are scientifically formulated for cats and they will definitely help you out during a crisis, but you will have to supplement their food with fresh meat. Perhaps you should keep Impala – they are not known as MacDonald's for lions for no reason." Fiona choked on her tea.

"No, I hate hunting and the killing of wildlife!" she cried. "What am I going to do? What am I going to do?"

"You could start a rabbit or a chinchilla farm …" Harry thought loudly.

"That is just as bad! I can imagine all those rabbits running around and being ripped apart by the lions. It is grotesque. There must be a better way!" Fiona became very agitated, got up and walked to the window that was covered with burglar bars and protected by security cameras befitting a Johannesburg organisation. "I have made my decision," she said "since I started feeding my Sam that Optimum Care and Whiskers, he had lost interest in the birds in my garden. He became a proper domesticated cat. I will do the same with the lions. Did you know that Whiskers belongs to the people who make Mars Bars? They must know how to make cat food delicious, just like they know how to make delicious chocolates. I shall write to them as soon as I get home

44

and ask for their advice. In the meantime, you better arrange for those bags of kibbles to be delivered to me. And remember – I want a decent variety – you cannot expect the lions to eat the same thing every day."

Printing an invoice for the produce took at least another hour. Shelley made wheezing noises through her nose, mumbled incoherently and made curious zigzag movements with the mouse on her coffee-stained mousepad while selecting the correct product items on her stock lists. When she was done, she printed a single page with the outstanding amount for Fiona to settle.

"Are you out of your fucking mind!" she screamed at Shelley.

"Do you know how many of those Taiwanese sweatshop dresses I am going to have to sell to be able to afford this food? Why don't I get special discounts? You know this is big business for you! Why don't you come to the party? I have been loyal to you all these years and now you screw me sideways in my moment of weakness! I insist that you come up with better prices!"

Fiona went blood red. One of those reds that started like a rash between her breasts, then crept up along her neck, all over her ears and into her face. Beads of sweat formed on her forehead as she took her Fossil purse out of her Matewis Maree hand stitched shoulder bag. She had invested heavily in this venture and could not afford to make mistakes.

Harry phoned his suppliers, had hushed conversations and finally explained that there was not much he could do. The food was imported, the Rand was a disaster after the President fired the Minister of Finance and there were no good prospects for a better exchange rate.

Fiona was furious. "Well, damn the government, Whiskers and Mars Bars. For all I care they are all brown for the same reason," she said.

The Urbanol straightened her out sufficiently to hand over her platinum card without the slightest tremble. Her voice became soft, controlled and less vulnerable. "Get it delivered. You know my address. And I don't pay for deliveries. If you have a problem with that, speak to your therapist." She hesitated for a moment while Shelley released the security gate, then stepped outside and disappeared into the afternoon traffic.

The long journey through the mountains, past endless road works and five toll gates, gave her ample time to think. Everything went according to plan, but this food thing was going to be a big problem. She needed the food to be prepared somewhere else at a reasonable price. She was never going to admit to anybody that the Whiskers would bankrupt her and she was not even sure that it would be good enough. Perhaps she should buy shares in the Mars Company? No, that would be stupid - she still had the exchange rate issue. These thoughts churned and churned in her head. Her mind eventually drifted to the meeting she had with the village folk. She remembered how she said to them: "The key to our success is that we have to stand together" and then the penny dropped. The answer to her predicament was simply to involve her neighbours. There was bound to be someone that could come up with a solution that did not involve killing animals at random for everyone to see and the most likely one would be Jean-Henri Desfourneaux.

By the time she got home, she was exhausted but happy, very happy. She had a plan and she would make that scrawny old man help her out. She poured herself a stiff Gin and Tonic, stretched out on her couch and relaxed for the first time in many days.

By the time the motorcycles arrived at the foot of the hill, Fiona was waiting for them in her silver Land Rover. Once they passed, she followed them, which placed her directly in front of the container truck with the two lions from the Kruger Park. Following the truck were Harry, the veterinarian, with three Parks Board assistants in his ageing four by four, a couple of white cars loaded with press photographers and finally, a large truck with brightly coloured Whiskers branding.

Opposite the Cheerio Chicken farm they turned onto a dirt road that snaked through the rain forest and finally to Fiona's lion farm. Nestled amongst the trees was the magnificent new reception building that was completed just in time. It resembled a giant insect with an undulated arched roof on steel pillar legs. The building was so cleverly designed and constructed of glass and supporting beams that it was almost invisible. The roof was clad with solar tiles, specially designed and imported from the Tesla Company to not only blend with the forest canopy but also generate all the electricity for the lion hospital, the fences and the visitors' areas. The building straddled and concealed a large underground parking area that doubled up as a storm water catchment surface which fed into a fresh water reservoir.

"I don't want to see any cars," Fiona said to the architect. "I don't ever want this place to look like a shopping mall with millions of cars around it at the end of the month." In the end they agreed to also provide a shuttle service from the village for visitors. The shuttle arrival kiosk was built below ground, adjacent to a large staircase connected to the ground floor level. Due to its high elevation, visitors could look down upon the roaming space, the canopy rides and the horizon in the distance. In addition, the ground floor level provided accommodation for a reception area, a restaurant, a bar and a shop with memorabilia.

To the right of the building was the entrance to the lion camps. Fiona had an enormous art nouveau style iron gate, like the ones she saw on the Paris Metro, made with the name 'Panthera Park' woven into the botanical patterns. Beyond the main gate was a second motorised gate. Only once the main gate was securely closed could the second one be opened to make sure that the cats would not escape when vehicles were given access to the property. Infrared cameras were positioned everywhere to monitor the movement of vehicles, visitors, workers and the precious cats.

For the occasion, Fiona enlisted the services of the people from Big Concerts to erect a temporary stage with a seating arrangement for people from the neighbourhood to witness the release of the first lions at Panthera Park. She parked her Land Rover next to the stage and ran to the main gate, where the truck with the lions came to a standstill. The vets and the reporters were directed to the underground parking and after a short while emerged through the main doors of the insect looking building. They carried all the tools of their trades with them. The vets had rucksacks with medication and emergency equipment; the reporters had laptops, cameras and tripods.

"Ugh, I'm so happy you made it!" Fiona cried. "How are my babies?"

Harry untied the tarpaulin that covered the side of the container and pealed it back to look inside. It was dead quiet. He turned to Fiona. "These lionesses are certainly no babies. They are old and will need special care."

"That's not a problem, they will have a very protected home here." Fiona was so excited she could not stand still. She was, as usual, dressed for the occasion – this

49

time in green tight fitting camouflage pants, knee high black leather riding boots, which she bought at the Tack Shop, and a beige tailored low cut t-shirt with 'Panthera Park' printed across the shoulders in an Art Nouveau font. Her mother's charm bracelet jingled around her arm every time she adjusted her hair or moved her Jackie O sunglasses to her forehead. Her appearance was exquisitely complimented by a caramel and vanilla aura of Opium Black fragrance which she applied lavishly that morning. Her trusted hand stitched Matewis Maree shoulder bag, filled with essentials such as nail file, slim line cigarettes, wallet, fragrance, touch-up makeup, telephone and a little lace handkerchief was, as usual, clutched under her arm or strapped over her shoulder.

"Well," she said, "what is the time now? I arranged with the village folk to be here at 9:00 o'clock for the formal release of the girls. What do you need to do before then?"

"They are still sleepy from the tranquilisers I gave them last night," Harry replied. "I'll check them out first before I wake them up. The driver can then park the truck next to the ramp so that they can get out. Everybody is exhausted after the long journey. Perhaps we should relax for a few minutes and have a coffee before we get going?"

At that very moment, Minnie from the waffle shop arrived with trays of food and coffee. She, like the rest of the village, was on standby since early that morning. When she heard the procession going past, she loaded her Kia SUV and drove the short distance to Panthera Park.

A while later, Fiona, Troy, Harry and the rest of the team sat down to have breakfast. In the distance, two workers loaded the purpose built silo with Whiskers kibbles. A conveyor belt was installed to deliver the kibbles to two large cement bowls in the centre of the viewing area. During the final couple of hours before the big event, the IT people from Incredible Erections managed to get all the cameras satellite connected to a live feed on Facebook and the Panthera Park website.

When Harry signalled that he was ready to proceed with the release process, the truck with its precious cargo slowly proceeded through the gates and parked next to the offloading ramp. At the same time the visitors started to arrive. All the village folk and the shop owners were there – Matthew from the brewery, Minnie from the restaurant, Liesie Strydom, the retired matron, Mary Johnson, who owned the chemist, the ladies from the Presbyterian Church, Paul from the Spit and Polish and off course Jean-Henri Desfourneaux, the funeral director and mayor of the village who also had a large chicken farm that was decimated by Newcastle disease.

At exactly 8:50 a.m. Fiona positioned herself behind the podium in front of the spectators. She started to tremble violently a few minutes earlier, but successfully squeezed an Urbanol out of the blister pack in her Matewis Maree hand stitched shoulder bag and surreptitiously put it between her lips. She then took a little sip of water from the bottle that was left at the podium for her by the event organisers. She turned around to look for a signal from Harry. He injected the lions with an antidote which started to take effect. They woke up and tried to get up, but quickly fell over again. Fiona opened her bag, took her iPhone out and logged into Facebook. There, right in front of her eyes she could see live streaming of the event. One of the reporters walked around the vehicle and filmed how the lions woke up. Then she saw Harry on her little monitor with a broad smile and a thumb up. It was his queue. She got up, adjusted her T-shirt and cleared her throat.

"Ladies and gentlemen, welcome." she said in a hushed voice. "Please do not applaud or make a noise. We do not want the lions to be scared, so please remain as quiet as possible while we set these girls free. This is a momentous occasion. Today we introduce our two lions to their new home. They will be able to live here for the rest of their lives and you can come to visit them as often as you like. We went to great lengths to create viewing space for you that will allow you to watch them in a normal habitat. If all goes well, they will soon be joined by a number of other lions that have been freed from circuses and zoos all over the world."

Fiona became overwhelmed with emotion. The reporter with the camera walked straight up to her to get a full frame image. In a quivering voice she added: "Our proceedings, even though they are in almost complete silence, are visible in every corner of the world. We want everyone out there to know that we see our wildlife as our heritage. We don't have fabulous buildings, art, cathedrals or sites of archaeological importance, but we have wildlife entrusted to us in this country for protection. We will make sure that they are protected here in the forest and we will make use of renewable energy that is not harmful to our environment. For that reason, we made use of consultants provided to us - free of charge - by the inimitable Mr Elon Musk. His personal endorsement is framed and available for view in the restaurant. We owe him and his organisation a huge debt of gratitude."

She wiped a tear of joy and accomplishment off her one eye while carefully keeping her red fingernail away from the soft tissue. Each member of the audience now looked at their telephone, voyeuristically following her every move.

She thanked Harry, the veterinarian and his assistants for their help and commitment as well as a list of other people and concerns, too many to list here. Finally, she concluded her speech with a statement.

"I am proud to announce our new debit card, the Indulge Card, in support of this initiative. It is accredited and underwritten by the major international clearing houses. If you do what I tell you to do, you will save a considerable amount of money on your normal banking transactions and at the same time support our lions. As you can imagine, we desperately need financial support for this initiative. Until now, everything you see here came out of my pocket."

She reached for her purse and took out a bank card which she held out to the camera, so that the world could see.

There was a gasp in the audience. They all knew that Fiona was literally and figuratively well heeled, but entering the world of banking was big-time stuff which they never dreamt she could pull off.

"I urge you to go to our website and fill in the application form. We have people on standby who will send your card to you anywhere in the world" she concluded. Before anyone could clap hands, she sat down and turned her attention to the lions.

As if on cue the first lion stood up and peered through the cage. Harry and the people from the Parks Board climbed on top of the container, unhooked the locking latches and readied themselves to set the lions free. When Harry gave the signal, they lifted the entire side panel. The tension in the air was so palpable that even the birds stopped singing.

At least three cameramen from the newspapers had their cameras pointed at the lions through the fence, their eyes glued to the view finders and right fingers on the trigger releases. Rays of sunlight streamed through the foliage as it did for thousands of years before. The forest was ready to welcome its children back.

The two lionesses got up. They groaned, looked at the open space and slowly walked to the edge of the cage. They stopped for a moment.

The conveyer belt started to run. From where we were sitting, we could see Whiskers kibbles of all colours pouring into the feeding bowls. The lions sniffed in the air and walked straight to the vessels where they stuck their noses into the kibbles. At first they just smelled and licked at the food pellets as if there was coloured water in their bowls. After a while, they must have realised that it was weird, but very tasty fast food because within minutes, they devoured large mouthfuls of kibbles.

By the time they had enough, they rubbed themselves against a strangle fig tree, rolled around on the grass and played with one another. The sound of camera shutters clicked relentlessly at every move the lions made. They captured exactly what everyone wanted to see - colourful images of lions in their own habitat, feeding on fast food for felines against the backdrop of a rain forest,

55

illuminated by rays of light through what remained of the morning mist.

Hundreds of viewers commented on Facebook. Little hearts were showered over the streamed images and likes tallied into thousands within minutes. Hits on the website skyrocketed and Indulge Card applications jammed the email server. The event was a resounding success. Fiona and her lions instantly became world famous. By 10 a.m. that morning, the newspaper reporters compiled articles and pictures which they transmitted around the globe from the hotspot that was especially assembled at Panthera Park.

One always needs a good story to kick a marketing strategy into gear. Fiona exploited the lions perfectly, with apparent sensitivity and boundless compassion to generate money and more money. By lunch time that day, the lion release videos were trending on YouTube and the afternoon newspapers had lead stories with an image of the lions rubbing themselves against a tree.

That afternoon, when she drove home, Fiona listened to the business news on the radio. The most significant share price increase for the day belonged to the Mars Company, it was reported.

Chapter 4

Hanging with Matthew

The knock on my door made me jump.

I was getting ready for a power nap after a long sun soaked afternoon at the village swimming pool. There was nobody around which made me confident enough to just lie there, deliciously lazy, worshiping the sloth god. At the end of the day, I gathered my things and went back to my cottage. By the time I got home, I headed straight for the shower.

The water energised me. I poured soft soap in my hand and spread it all over my body, taking particular care of my nose and finger tips. After I rinsed my face, I sat down under the water jet, crossed my legs and washed between my toes. The last remaining bits of old skin exfoliated as I washed the soap away, leaving me shiny and youthful as the day I was born. I dried my body with a soft white towel and walked back to my room. There, I stood in front of my bed, cupped my hand and filled it with moisturising liquid which I applied all over my chest, arms and belly. I watched in the mirror how the moisturiser disappeared into my skin, revealing my darkening tan and geometric patterns from the top of my hands to the curve of my shoulders. Years of dedicated gym training gave me well defined arms with distinct v-shapes in my triceps. Nestled in these curves were growing monochrome shapes I would never have chosen, but which I loved. Thin, almost translucent, grey horizontal lines across the square shapes of my chest graduated to darker grey stripes at the base of my abdomen. I took a handful of moisturiser, rubbed it between my palms and applied it between my legs, around my scrotum and via the little treasure trail to my navel. My skin was super sensitive and tingles rippled through my body which made me horny. I had almost forgotten what that felt like. I had been alone for such a long time.

"Are you in there, bro?"

I had just enough time to cover myself with a towel before Matthew opened the door.

"What's up brother?" he said with a big grin.

I blushed and tried not to look startled or caught in the act.

"I've come to fetch you so that you can be at the planning meeting tonight. We're gonna kick some ass."

"Sure, let me get dressed quickly," I said and turned around.

"Wow, you look awesome bro," he said.

"What do you mean?"

"Wow, the ink on your back is rad! The shapes look like those on my original breeding pair. All I can say is you look super sick."

"Really?" I asked. "I can only see the front of my body in this mirror."

"Give me that cream. Let me put some on your back. You look a little burnt," he said.

Holding the bottle high above my shoulders he squirted blobs of cream in the valley between my shoulders. He then flattened his hands against my back, moved them up, around the contours of my shoulders and down, with outstretched thumbs, as guides against my spine, until he cupped my hips firmly. I did my best not to respond, but when he suddenly, locked his arm round my neck from behind and trawled his free hand through my ass, my knees lost their firmness, and I forgot, for a moment, where I was, who I was and who was with me.

"We must go," Matthew said. "We must not be late. There's going to be fun and games tonight. We cannot let that bitch of a Fiona get away with all the spoils."

I quickly put on my undies, slipped into my jeans, secured them with a leather belt and stretched into a black t-shirt. On the way out, I flung my dirty clothes over the stupid mannequin, grabbed a beanie, my wallet, cigarettes and slipped my feet into a pair of slops next to the front door.

The evening was still young, but it was almost pitch dark. A warm, early summer wind stirred the last leaves on the road. There were clouds in the sky, almost invisible in the dark, but one could tell because they obscured the stars and there was a familiar smell of rain in the air. We walked next to one another; he with his skater boy looks in his long shorts, powerful calves that reached into his Van's shoes with secret socks, hooded jacket and blond dreads that flipped untidily around his shoulders as carefree as the leaves under our feet. I felt comfortable with him. I was new here and he took the trouble to make me feel at home. I trusted him.

By the time we got to the Spit and Polish most of the locals were there. Matthew ordered a couple of Viper Premiums and found a bench seat for us at the back of the room. A few candles provided sufficient light for us to be inconspicuous, yet present. Most of the people were so busy getting pissed they did not even notice us. I thought it was rather curious that it was only the two of us who drank Viper beer – the rest of the crowd drank the usual stuff you could buy in the city.

"Good evening ladies and gentlemen," it was the creaky, nasal voice of Jean-Henri Desfourneaux.

"Tonight we are going to discuss how to make the village a haven for lonely people," he said.

Desfourneaux parked himself in front of the Darth Vader fireplace, which was apparently in hibernation. The clipboard in his hand contained a few scribbles which he, no doubt, wanted to share with the audience relative to Fiona's mind map which was fixed to the wall behind him.

"Don't underestimate that old dude," Matthew said in my ear. "He comes from a pretty weird family. His old man was the last French executioner that killed people in public. When you have a chance, Google his surname."

"Seriously?"

"Yeah, he and his folks came from a long line of executioners named Desfourneaux stretching back many hundreds of years. Apparently they all chopped people's heads off with a guillotine. Can you imagine growing up in a house like that and going to town with your old man to see what work he did?"

I laughed out loudly. "That must have been the most disciplined household in the word. I'm sure his wife and children never argued with him."

"Make sure your rooms are clean and tidy, or you'll go to work with daddy tomorrow." Matthew was on a roll.

We laughed behind our hands like two naughty schoolboys. On the other side of the room the mayor made announcements and welcomed people to the proceedings.

"Apparently his old man was one of the only executioners who was ever filmed doing an execution. The fucking French are so faulty. I believe after that particular execution they had such a wild party at the jail that the authorities moved executions behind closed doors. It was hectic bro, think about it, on execution day they killed some asshole and then the whole city partied throughout the night to jazz bands and French wine. I'm sure they made quite a few execution babies too, like we make on New Year's or Christmas." Matthew giggled next to me and made curious zigzag movements with his legs on the bench next to me.

"Bro, that is a macabre thought." I bumped Matthews' shoulder with mine and looked at Desfourneaux. I followed his gestures, his speech and his frame as he paced up and down, pointing at things and talking to the locals. There was no life in him. His eyes were so deeply sunken that only shadowy patches remained above the bony arches of his cheeks. Regardless if he had shaven, his cheeks always seemed to be covered in a blue beard residue that was much heavier than a five o'clock shadow. It weighed his face down to a pinched snarl that left just enough room for two buck teeth. Liesie said to me that nobody ever saw his lower teeth - not even when he once smiled after the funeral of that sweet Mrs Green, who bequeathed her enormous property next to the funeral parlour to him because he was so kind to her during the last days of her life. If it wasn't for her, he

64

would never have been able to build the chapel in the middle of the village where all the weddings and funerals were held.

"Rumour has it that his father killed quite a number of famous people before he eventually went insane and subsequently died. Since the French abolished the death sentence, our Mr Desfourneaux didn't have a job and came to live here instead." Matthew rolled his eyes. "The thing is," he said, "I don't believe the apple has fallen far from the tree in this case. That old bastard knows exactly what he is doing. He is all over the old people at the old age home like a bad rash and I'm sure he makes a lot of money out of them. Cunning old bastard!"

Matthew held his beer out to me and clinked against mine. He winked, sipped on his drink and smiled.

"Is this seat taken?" A girl, probably in her mid-twenties, pointed at a chair next to us.

"I don't think so." I said.

"Sit down! Make yourself comfortable. I'm Matthew. What's your name?" He held a fist out to her. She did not know how to respond, so she sat down, giggling. "Thank you. [giggle] I'm Candy. [giggle] What's happening here? Is there gonna be a band playing? [giggle] I just walked in here and don't know this place."

Oh no, I thought. This blow-up doll on steroids was going to drive me insane.

Matthew leant over to me and said: "I'm gonna fuck her tonight."

He rubbed the bulge in his pants and grinned at me. "What do you say, we both fuck her?" He put his hand between my legs. I was so taken aback by the sudden change of topic and events that I had, what I can best describe as a momentary intellectual arrest. The kind of thing you saw on George Bush's face when he was told that a plane flew into the World Trade Centre. I just looked straight ahead, like the president. The circumstances that unfolded around me, exposed all my insecurities. I leant over to Matthew and whispered:

"I have never fucked a girl," I blushed and looked at the floor.

"I gathered that much from the first evening we spent together," he said, "but with me around, I promise you will have no problem with her." I could see how his eyes glowed in the dark, fixed on his prey.

The tension was broken momentarily when Desfourneaux called everyone to order: "I trust that you all have a drink. May I ask for recommendations from the floor to get this meeting started?"

"Yes, I would like to make a couple of suggestions." It was Paul from the Spit and Polish. "I think we need to change the way people think about our village. It is well known as a place for the newly wed and the nearly dead. That is not the kind of place where people are likely to find friends or romance."

"So, what do you suggest?"

"Well, I think we all know about Trip Advisor. We must stay away from them as far as possible because we don't want to attract those kind of people. I think we must link up with the websites where people can hook up like Tinder and Grindr, affiliate with them and offer our village as a permanent hook-up venue. In other words, we can become a village with benefits." Everybody laughed as Paul sat down. In a bizarre way, it made sense and they all knew it.

When I looked towards the entrance, I saw a woman walking towards the group. She looked fidgety and irritable. It was Fiona. She sat down and waved at the bartender with the big breasts in her usual undersized t-shirt. A short while later I saw her delivering a drink and a napkin. Fiona removed the umbrella from the glass, pealed a straw from its container and took a sip.

"What are Tinder and Grindr?" Desfourneaux wanted to know. "I don't understand."

Matthew and Candy shrieked with laughter.

"It's, for want of a better expression, an Internet version of a lonely hearts club where people can meet and get to know each other," Paul explained amidst raucous laughter. "Perhaps you should create a profile for yourself – you might just get lucky!"

I could see Desfourneaux interpreted the laughter as a slight at him. His body language became stiff and remained speechless until Minnie raised her hand. "I agree with Paul," she said. "Those are the perfect marketing avenues for us. It will not cost us much and we will immediately reach more people than on Facebook. What we have to do next is to upgrade our individual businesses with our target market in mind."

"What do you suggest?" Desfourneaux wanted to know again.

"Well, we seriously have to upgrade the places where people can stay." Minnie replied. "Before I came here, I went for a walk through some of our cottages and rooms. Most of them are old and in desperate need of improvement. I think we must all agree that we will have the rooms fixed up. And we have to make sure that the beds are decent. Some of the beds I've tried are like hammocks with warn out Mr Price linen. We have to do better than that."

"That's all good and well to say, but how are we going to afford that? We already see less people coming here and I am on the verge of making a loss with my cabins. I cannot agree with this." We all looked at Trudie. She had a hard time getting over the death of her husband a year ago. Her health was also not great.

"Don't worry about the money for now. Let's understand what we need to do and then see if we can raise the funds to get it done. I agree with Minnie, we cannot expect people to come and stay here and have them sleep on shagged out beds covered in fucking autumnal colours. Come to think of it, most of you were probably conceived on those beds. It's time to make a bonfire and make a few improvements." Everyone turned to Fiona on the other side of the room. I loved watching her having a drag on one of those Vogue extra length slender cigarettes, hollowing her cheeks and then exhaling while waving her hand away from her face. Fabulously theatrical, I thought and grinned.

Matthew paid no attention to the discussion. "Let's have a Tequila!" Before either of us could say anything he signalled the breasts to bring us three double golds. The drinks arrived on a round tray that must have seen many moments of broken resistance.

"Here you go," Matthew said to Candy, who giggled again and handed her a large tot glass. We clinked our glasses and downed our drinks. Matthew and I washed ours down with Vipers. Candy lost her giggle for a moment as the tequila burnt its way down her throat.

"Here, have some of my lemon." I held a slice of lemon out to her. She bit into it and wrapped her lips around my fingers as she sucked up the drops. Matthew looked at me and smiled. I knew what he was thinking.

"If we want people to meet and become acquainted, we have to create a space where everybody can get together informally," Paul suggested. "I think we should clear the square between the pub and the restaurants, pave that area and put large tents up so that people can have an informal gathering space. We can serve them from the existing kitchens at the open areas. Then we can invite bands to play there and make it a fun place to be. The village hall is much too formal and old fashioned. Nobody wants to go there."

"I agree with Paul," Matthew responded. "It will be much cheaper to do that than upgrading the village hall. We can organise a cheese and craft beer fair every now and again. We can even get the weirdos here to do a holistic fair. That is certain to bring lots of lonely visitors. Once they are here, we can take them on outings to Troy's place, the lions and our place, where we make beer. I promise you, I'll feed them enough beer to make them fall in love." Everybody laughed at Matthew. "Boom!" He said, "Let's make it happen. We can make this the coolest place around."

"If we are all in agreement, then the next step is to work out the costs," Fiona said. "The good news is that the Indulge Card is working well and many people from around the world have signed up after the first lions were released at Panthera Park. I'm not really supposed to do this, but we can always take a little loan against the money people have put into their accounts. Then we can get this place jacked up and also pay the loan back in good time." Everybody in the room went quiet. Nobody ever expected Fiona to be such an ingenious money manipulator and such a generous business partner.

"That is on one condition." Fiona said. "No fucking Mr Price Home. We will not have guest lodges that look like shop showrooms. If you want to buy there – you are on your own."

"Well, if there is nothing else to discuss, then I think we can close the formalities and enjoy ourselves," Desfourneaux said.

"Yeah," Mathew said, "more tequila. How's your beer bro?"

"Finished."

"What can I get you to drink Candy?" he asked.

"Oh, [giggle] can I have a vodka, passion fruit and lemonade?"

"Sure!" he said and waved at the breasts.

"Max, I want to talk to you and the old man please." To my surprise Fiona was standing in front of me.

"Sure Fiona." I said and followed her. She called Desfourneaux and we sat down on the quiet side of the pub. She fumbled in her bag for a cigarette.

"Jean-nie, you and I are both screwed," she said. "Those bloody lions are besotted with the Whiskers. They're like orphan children with a bag of doughnuts. It's a fucking nightmare. Almost all the Whiskers I bought for their release is finished. I cannot afford to keep buying and buying." Desfourneaux and I looked at each other.

"I spent a gigantic amount of money on that farm. Just the architect almost bankrupted me. I cannot afford to keep spending so much money on food every month. If the Brits approve of the venue, there will be another twelve lions on route here soon."

"Don't give me such a smug look you old asshole. You are not any better off. That chicken farm of yours is ruined after the Newcastle disease. So, I have a plan. I can get us a meat crusher machine at the cold meat manufacturers in the city. They use it to crush bones and meat and all the shit they put into polony. If I buy a machine like that and the press that comes with it, we can install the contraption at your chicken farm, crush up all your sick chickens and also get all the animals that die of natural causes around here, put them through the machine and make our own Whiskers. And come to think of it, with this listeria hysteria, the polony business is equally fucked, so I should get one for a good price."

Desfourneaux clearly loved the idea. "How much will you pay me for my chickens?" he wanted to know.

"I'm not paying you for your diseased chickens! They are worthless. But we can partner in the kibble business. I'm sure we can sell food to other sanctuaries too - even the Kruger Park during droughts."

"And why am I here?" I asked. "I don't know anything about these things."

"Max," Fiona said, "I know you want to get out of the city. You have been a great client over the years, but I think it is time you make this your home now. I think you will be perfect to help Troy manage this kibble making operation. I'll make sure we buy equipment that will automate the process as far as possible so that we can put a carcass in on the one side and get kibbles out on the other side. And I'll make sure the food pellets are a decent size. Normal Whiskers pellets are too small. We need to give the lions nice big crunchy kibbles that will keep their teeth clean and healthy."

"Wow, Fiona, I'm not so sure about that. Matthew asked me to do work for him at the brewery as well."

"Ok, think about it. It might be a new career for you. Did you know that Whiskers belongs to Mars Bars? It is a global organisation with incredible wealth. Perhaps one day we will be as big as they are."

"I certainly will." I said goodbye and went back to Matthew and the bimbo.

Matthew was a fast mover. When I got to them, he was sitting sideways on our bench facing Candy. There was an empty round of glasses on the table and mine was waiting for me. Candy's spine was almost as limp as her eyelids.

"I cannot drink that on my own," I said. "Let me order a last round for the two of you."

"Two double tequilas," I signalled to the breasts.

"And one whole lemon with the rind removed," Matthew shouted.

When the drinks arrived, Matthew explained a new trick. We had to down our drinks and share the lemon with him. So we clinked our glasses and downed our tequila. Matthew held the lemon in his mouth and the two of us locked lips with him to share the lemon. He held our faces tightly in his arms. Our tongues touched in a three-way kiss that tasted of liquor, cigarettes and citrus. I, again, briefly lost touch with reality.

"Are you going to fuck me?" Candy giggled.

"You bet! We both are." Matthew said. "Let's go home and get naked."

Chapter 5

Skin Deep

The lights dimmed for hard core hour at the Spit and Polish.

That meant that it was time for the last drinks of the night. Across the road from the pub was the police station. They did not care if people drank themselves into a different blood group, as long as the pub did not sell alcohol after 2 a.m. The police could enforce the alcohol sales hours, but it was pointless trying to pursue the patrons. They all lived within walking distance from the pub or just a short drive back to their homes.

Deep house music filled the pub with a deliciously funky beat.

"Someone to count on in a world ever changin'.
Here I am, stop where you standin'.
What you need is a lover, a man to take over.
Oh baby don't look any further."

Matthew took care of the practical things. He disappeared behind the bar, settled the bill and returned with cigarettes, a bottle of tequila gold, a six-pack of Vipers and a six-pack of Smirnoff Ice. Just as well, I did not want Candy to get stuck in the Vipers. That was our domain.

"Party time guys!" he shouted from across the tables with a huge smile and a lapdog tongue. "Let's get our asses out of here!"

On our way out, I saw Desfourneaux slumped in a chair, fast asleep. Not a pretty sight, I thought. He looked like a heap of dirty washing in a corner. I didn't want to grow old like that.

The rhythm remained in our bones. The short walk to my cottage in the soft rain was fun. There was great energy in the air. Sexual energy. Candy was sufficiently pissed to babble non-stop at a pitch that could cut through a cheesecake. And that awful laugh of hers was certainly perilous to the workings of the streetlights. Every now and again one dimmed and came back on. The village was dead quiet at that time of the morning, apart from our footsteps on the gravel and her incessant giggling. All I wished for, was for the bloody bitch to keep quiet. Matthew presumably had the same idea, because he grabbed her from behind, turned her head and kissed her. That shut her up and saved the moment.

It was obvious why Matthew wanted to get into her. She was pretty, with dark eyes and naturally sculptured eyebrows that responded every time she laughed. Her facial features were framed by an abundance of dark brown, almost reddish hair that untidily flopped on her shoulders. She was super slender, with little green tomato tits and an abdomen so tiny, I wondered where she saved all the drink she consumed throughout the evening. She reminded me of the physical confidence I noticed among the dancers I got to know when I had a fling with a ballet dancer. Matthew easily wrapped his arm around her waist and playfully lifted her up. She responded with a yelp that got every dog in the neighbourhood going. She was no angel. That was certain. She was much too relaxed considering what was about to happen. In fact, she was excited and encouraged Matthew to take control, not only with her, but with me too.

When we arrived at my place, the rain came down strongly. It was cold in the middle of summer, so I woke Darth Vader from his hibernation and made a fire. Matthew poured us tequilas which we washed down with Vipers. Candy took a large gulp of her Ice. I plugged my iPhone into the sound system and selected my Goldfish playlist. When I turned around, Candy was sitting on the edge of the bed and Matthew was on his knees in front of her. I watched them kissing – he was quiet and deliberate, she was subservient but responsive.

"Come here," Matthew said. He pushed Candy backward on the bed and me on top of her. "Taste her mouth."

While we kissed, Matthew took our shoes off and pulled my pants down my legs. I could feel his hands all over my ass, then on my shoulders. It was deliciously seedy.

"Smoke break," he announced and got up. I followed him and stood next to the bed. He took a large gulp of his beer and offered me some too. We lit cigarettes and stared at Candy who was lying on her back.

"I want to watch you undress each other," she said.

Without a word Matthew pulled my t-shirt off. I did the same for him. I then went on my knees, grabbed his shorts by the bottoms and pulled them down. It was the first time I saw him naked. I wrestled out of my own underwear as I got up.

"Oh my god!" Candy shrieked. "You have the same tats! Look at you! Wow that is so weird."

We laughed.

"I want a spliff - this is gonna be something else!"

She fumbled in her bag for paraphernalia to make a blunt. Within less than a minute she had a drag of her expertly rolled joint.

"Last round," Matthew said to me. "Down your beer. We are going to Neverland. This is going to be the best sex you have ever had."

The tequila, cigarettes and beer took me on a trip. My vision became a series of images that faded in and out through black, but my sensations accelerated in waves of incredible, sometimes even excruciating sensitivity that was single-mindedly propelled by primordial instinct. I was aware of Candy and Matthew next to me, aware of their nakedness and embraced the moment.

Candy was super fucked by then. The blunt removed every last element of resistance she might have had. All she needed was to be immersed in her own mindless world of decadence and submission. How she got out of her clothes I don't know.

I watched Matthew on top of her. When she tried to squeal, he put his mouth over hers. The noisier she became, the firmer he held her. In the end, all I could hear were muffled noises. When she calmed down a little, he twisted her shoulders so that the three of us could get our mouths together. We kissed and rode the wave to Neverland.

In the darkness I noticed how Matthew's tongue became forked and how he used it to fathom new depths in Candy's mouth and between her legs. She responded with gasps and sighs, but he did not seem to notice.

The predator got his prey.

Matthew's convulsions were sudden. Almost casually, he arched backwards with his mouth wide open in a yawn that almost dislocated his jaw.

"Uhm, uhm …" he mumbled. In a flash, he lunged forward and bit into Candy's neck. There was just enough light from the fireplace to see that his skin turned dull and his eyes opaque. His arms searched for me and his lips found mine. We held on to each other until we fell asleep.

Outside, the rain came down in buckets. Heavy thunder and flashes of lightning woke me sometime later. Matthew stood next to me. He was naked except for his boxer shorts. I tried to cover myself, but he pulled the bed covers away from me.

"There is big shit bro."

"What happened?"

"The bitch is dead."

"What do you mean?" I sat upright.

"It's bad bro. She is really dead."

"Don't be crazy! Come back to bed."

"No seriously bro, she is dead. When I woke up, the door was wide open and she was lying there - ice cold. Look there she is. I threw a blanket over her."

I looked towards the door. The fire had died, but in the last candle light and the occasional lightning I could see her on her back.

My first thought was - just as well, humanity was saved from that insufferable voice, but then I panicked and thought that even a rooky forensic detective would find my body fluids all over her. It was a wild shag, but not so hectic that we killed her! How was this possible?

My buddy also panicked. "This is fucked up bro. This is not cool at all. I did not know rigour mortis happened so quickly. She is ice cold and stiff and revolting to touch. It was the first time that I touched a dead person." He cringed and shivered. "Have a look …"

Before he could lift the blanket, I said: "Fuck no! I don't want to look at her or touch her. Why the fuck did she die Matthew? Are you sure she is dead? I saw you biting her …"

"Look bro, things got a little out of hand last night. We were a little out of it and yes, I bit her in the neck. I'm sorry, it was a reflex. My eyes are weird these days. By the way, can you see things in the dark yet? I can see shapes in the dark if they are warm or hot and I react to them. I cannot help it. Talking about hot. Fuck bro, you were red hot last night. You really turned me on. The proof in the pudding is that I shed my skin which fucked up my eyes even more. That is the best ever, when you don't only get your rocks off but you lose your skin too. And the next morning, when you have a brand-new skin, there is nothing better than touching, playing and enjoying your body."

I remembered how turned on I was after spending the day at the swimming pool, how sensitive my nipples were and how Matthew almost caught me in the act.

"Would you like a beer?" He asked. "There are still a few in the fridge. Perhaps it will calm us down a little."

He opened two Vipers for us. We went outside and had a cigarette. The rain stopped. There was a smell of cleanliness in the air blended with the aroma of crab apple flowers.

"We will have to get her out of here before day breaks," I said. "I'm not sleeping with a dead body in the room."

"Ok brother, I have an idea. Let's put her on the back of the truck. We can take her to Desfourneaux's place. He has huge freezers at his chicken farm that are not being used after all his chickens died. Let's leave her there until we have a better plan."

We rolled Candy in two blankets for good measure. By then, she was as stiff as a plank, which made things a little easier. When we were ready, Matthew went outside to make sure there were no witnesses. We put Candy on the back of the truck, covered her with a few bags of garbage and set off to Cheerio. It was my first visit to the farm. Matthew, on the other hand, had been there on many occasions. He knew exactly where to go. The journey there felt like eternity.

We parked in front of a huge corrugated iron and brick building with massive doors. It was easy to slide the doors open. Inside were empty chicken coops. The place stank of chicken shit. Matthew surveyed the space with a flash light to make sure it was safe to take the body inside. We found a two-wheel trolley, loaded Candy, feet first and wheeled her through the empty space to a refrigeration unit adjacent to the main building.

Matthew opened the heavy fridge door to let me in. I wheeled Candy in and followed him to a rear corner filled with cardboard boxes.

"Here," he said, "nobody will find her here."

We put her on a shelf and stood there for a moment, uncertain what to do next. She was going to sleep in the cold, I thought, but she was at least warm under the blankets. Matthew made sure that she was neatly and securely positioned and stepped back. When I turned round to get out, I bumped against one of the cardboard boxes. It fell down. In the flash light I could see there was another frozen body, of a naked boy, in his early twenties.

"Who the hell is that?" I said.

"Don't worry about him. Since we don't have a morgue in the area, Desfourneaux leaves bodies here before he buries them or takes them to the crematorium next door. It is in any case too expensive for him to get the furnace going for one body at a time, so he usually waits for a while until he has a few bodies to burn before he gets the crematory going. We will just sneak her in amongst the others when the next batch gets cooked brother."

"Let's get out of here, I'm freaking out."

Before we left, I had a good look at that boy. I was convinced that he had teeth marks in his neck. We covered the corpses with cardboard boxes and closed the fridge door on our way out. Last, but not least, we took the trolley to where we found it.

The cool fresh air and beers we had before we drove to Cheerio knocked me in the face. The winding drive back to the village was nevertheless magical with more rain splashing against the windscreen. I stared at the animated white lines on the road that stretched past the truck. Sometimes there was a sign that screamed a message of caution. We listened to glorious funky music that made my body sway in rhythm and closed my eyes.

After all of that, we got back to my cottage just before daybreak.

With the body out of the way, we made a fresh fire, talked endlessly and fell asleep surrounded by music, crumpled up clothes and empty bottles.

The secrets of the night remained in the dark.

Chapter 6

Stairway to Heaven

The air of transformation was intoxicating.

The mayor, Mr Desfourneaux, assembled the few people who worked at the village office, for an emergency meeting. There were urgent items on the agenda. The sign at the turnoff from the freeway had to be replaced, the main entrance to the village had to be re-tarred, quotes were necessary to get the village square paved (provided that the old oak trees were not harmed in any way), covered with umbrellas and filled with seating, the park needed to be cleaned and a fresh electrical connection had to be installed to Cheerio, to power the new machinery Fiona acquired.

Following the plans that were made at the Spit and Polish, Fiona took the long journey back to the city in her Land Rover, on a mission to buy a meat processor and press. She was terrified. She started this venture and she now had to complete what she started, but she did not realise how much it would ultimately cost. Fortunately, this was the last major expense, but she had no previous experience with meat crushing machines. She tried to see how they worked on YouTube, but the process was so grisly that there was not a single video that showed exactly what happened inside those machines.

Importing a machine was no option with the Rand at an all-time low and the currency nearing junk status, so she opted for an alternative. She called up the processed meat manufacturers and asked if they had any equipment for sale. In the end she found a company that provided 'no name brand' polony to a few grocery stores, but lost their contract because unexplained ingredients, imported from South America, were found in their products. To make matters worse, when the cause of an outbreak of listeria was traced back to their polony, the company had to recall all their products. Faced with fatalities, legal liabilities and insolvency, they were keen to get rid of some of their assets and welcomed an opportunity to sell some of their heavy equipment.

On her way to the city, Fiona turned up the sound so that she could hear the Gregorian chant music better. She mumbled along with the melodies. Every now and again she opened the window, lit one of her Vogue extra slender cigarettes and stretched her fingers as she held the fag between her red fingernails.

Waze directed her to a warehouse close to the international airport in Jet Park. It was a miserable part of town. After all, who wanted to live at the end of the runway with planes flying in and out at all hours of the day and night? The houses were apparently built off a single plan, because they all looked like post-war variations on the same theme. Over many years unbridled decay set in. Strangely enough, even the home improvements looked like decaying structures, roughly fabricated from left-over materials scavenged somewhere else, without a thought spared for design, appearance or beauty. Filth and components hoarded to fix cars or to add that extra room for grandma, that never materialised, covered most of the available space on the properties. Yellow lawns that survived on rainwater, created a bleak expanse in front of some of the houses that were curiously also surrounded by chicken wire fences with farm gates that permanently remained ajar.

Filthy children with bare feet were playing with a soccer ball in the street accompanied by a few black dogs covered in mange. The streetlights were vandalised, presumably by the same children and their BB guns. Every globe cover hung free. Plastic bags mixed with dust tumbled in the gusts of wind across the road. Fiona felt as if ants, or rather, fleas were crawling up her legs as she drove down the street. Her airways choked up. She felt dirty and tarnished and asthmatic all at once. Her left hand instinctively reached into her Matewis Maree hand stitched bag for Ventolin and Urbanol. She sucked hard on the Ventolin dispenser and expertly dislodged a pill from the blister pack which she gulped down with a sip of water.

"At the roundabout, take the first exit. Your destination is on the left."

The Waze voice helped her focus. She screwed the cap on the water bottle and followed the instructions. Her destination turned out to be a large corrugated iron warehouse that was covered in rust, yet instantly recognisable by the two massive signs "Spider Brands" and "Energise Polony" at roof height.

Massive steel roller doors on either side of the building towered over paved areas marked 'Deliveries' and 'Dispatch'. Fiona could easily identify the office area by the two windows overlooking the street. She parked her Land Rover, got out, wiped her arms and legs with wet wipes (just in case there were really fleas) and adjusted her skirt. She was ready to negotiate.

One must admit that Fiona, even in her most insecure moments, came across as in control and she was, frankly, impressive. I suspect that a substantial amount of the credit belonged to big pharma, but she somehow managed to keep her shit together. That was certainly the impression that Mr Gupta had of her when she pushed the rotten plywood door open at the office of the Energise Polony Company. She looked at the curve of the scuff mark on the faded green linoleum floor with disgust and thought why did they not fix this fucking door years ago? There was nothing appetising about this place. The air in the office was thick with dust and smoke. Piles of lever arch files and paperwork were stacked on tables and on the floor. Mr Gupta raised from the chair behind his desk, littered with MacDonald's wrappers and in-trays that never emptied. He stared at Fiona over his reading glasses and hastily swallowed the last of his Quarter Pounder with Cheese. She could still excuse him for eating at work, but his pink shirt with yellow sweat stains under his arms, which she could smell from across the room, repulsed her instantly. His thick lips formed a big smile around his nicotine stained teeth.

"Welcome," he said. "You must be Mrs …" and held a hand out to her.

"Call me Fiona," she said, keeping her hand to herself. The feeling that fleas were crawling up her legs became very real.

"Sit down, I am very happy to meet you." He pushed an old fashioned typist chair in her direction. The one wheel did not work very well, so the thing screeched and tilted as he positioned it in front of the desk which was so full of papers that there was no room for Fiona to put her bag. She did not want to put it there anyway. One look at the cracked dark green vinyl seat made her imagine how many overweight secretaries had had their periods on that chair.

"Never mind the seat. I'm rather in a rush so please show me the machine. We can talk business along the way."

"Ok," he said and opened a double door that led into the production area.

There, in the middle of a tennis court green painted cement floor, stood the machine. Yellow stripes were painted on the floor approximately one meter away from the monster that rose like a steam locomotive out of the floor. It was covered in black louvered ventilation panels that made it look even more imposing.

At first Fiona was taken aback. What the hell did she get herself into? She slowly walked towards the monstrosity.

"Why are there yellow lines painted around the machine?" She asked.

"That is the safe area within which people may walk around the crusher."

"Oh."

"Let me show you how the whole process works." Mr Gupta said and walked to the other side of the contraption.

"This is where it all starts." He pointed to a conveyor belt with a big funnel that was positioned at the one end of the machine.

"This is where the ingredients go in. In our case, when we used to make polony, we premixed deboned chicken, pork, pork rind, vegetable protein and flavourings and then added everything in here into the grinder-mixer. You don't have to use deboned meat. This machine has an inbuilt crusher that will pulverise bones and cartilage.

94

Even bones the size of a cow skull will happily go through the machine. Once the meat and bones have been crushed and mixed, the ingredients will come out here as a thick paste, similar to that which you will find in a sausage filling."

Fiona wanted to vomit. She, nevertheless, followed Gupta from a distance, with a face that would have scared the children at the neighbouring primary school. He moved forward, opened a panel and pointed to a spout-like contrivance with a mini conveyer belt.

"The mixture comes out here and can be shaped in a variety of ways. We made sausages, but you can make patties or any other shape you prefer. You can also decide how smooth or chunky the mixture must be. The dispenser just needs a special plate to form the shapes you need. We can have one made for you across the road at the engineering works."

With reflux edging at the back of her throat, Fiona said: "This machine works just like an enormous version of my grandma's mincing machine," and swallowed hard. "I like it!"

She was not sure how much longer she could handle the situation and wanted to get it over with as quickly as possible. She had visions of animals being thrown into the machine alive, in a frenzy of butchery, coming out on the other side as biltong wagon wheels.

95

"Wait, you haven't seen the best part yet." Mr Gupta was excited. He could sense a deal coming on. "From here the conveyor belt goes into the oven. The mixture gets cooked here at a perfect temperature. When the product comes out the other side, it cools down in this section and then arrives there at the finished goods station." He walked to the place where the conveyer belt made its final appearance. "At the last station, the finished goods can be packaged and shipped to the warehouse or the client."

"It will do the trick, I think." Fiona said.

"Mr Gupta, we have a deal, on these conditions. You are going to sterilise this machine and then you are going to make me one bag of sample product to prove that this machine can do what you say it can. Yes, and you are going to go to the engineering business you talked about to have a plate made for me. I want the mixture to come out in the shape of a fully grown lion nail. When it is cooked, I want a large size crunchy kibble which my lions can eat. Just as well that the machine can chop up the bones, because we need a substantial amount of bone meal in the mixture."

"I'm sure it can be done Mrs ..."

"Yes, I am also sure. Now let's talk business. How old is this machine?" Fiona took her iPad out of her hand stitched Matewis Maree shoulder bag and started to type.

"Three years."

"So you have depreciated the machine over a period of five years, I guess?"

"Yes, correct."

"And the machine has gone through all its scheduled maintenance and cleaning services?"

"Yes, correct."

Fiona thought for a second then said: "In that case I offer you 15% of the original purchase price as a cash settlement and you must move this thing to my place free of charge." She then lifted her iPad and took a selfie with the machine in the background.

Before Gupta could open his mouth, she turned around and walked towards the door. She had enough of that place and needed to get out into the fresh air, or as fresh as one could get in this area. When she saw the grime on the door handle she hesitated, just enough for Gupta to catch up on her. He opened the door for her and said: "Mrs ..., I am just the accountant here on behalf of my cousins who left the country. It is my job to do the liquidation of the assets. We were hoping for a much better deal ..."

"Well that is all I can afford! You know as well as I do that the market for which you acquired that thing is as dead as the animals that found eternity through your business endeavours. So be my guest … find a better price."

Having said that, she kicked the front door open. She wanted to get out. How these people could make food for human consumption was beyond her. Never, never in her life will she look at processed meat in the supermarket again. She felt fleas all over her back crawling into the hairy curves of her neck. She choked and felt another asthma attack coming on.

"Call me tomorrow morning. My offer is valid for 24 hours only," were the last words Mr Gupta heard as he stared at her getting into the safety of her Land Rover.

As she sped away, she called Desfourneaux while frantically cleaning herself with a fresh batch of wet wipes.

"Listen Jan'nie, I bought a kibble machine for a song. This listeria hysteria could not have happened at a better time! You better get that place of yours in order so that it can be installed. Get Troy and Matthew to help you. And don't forget about the electrical connections to your farm. I hope you did not forget …."

"Yes Fiona, I'll make sure everything is prepared," he said full well that he had not started with anything.

"I cannot come back today," she said, "my Land Rover needs a service and I have to run a few errands in the city, but I will be back in the next day or so."

"Very well Fiona, travel safely," he said and ended the call.

It was at that moment that Desfourneaux called the emergency meeting. He never, even for a moment, thought that things would happen so quickly. Putting up a sign and paving the square would not take that much effort, but repairing the old chicken building, strengthening the floor and installing the new machine with its conveyor belts would be time consuming. He rushed through the agenda and task list with the few people in the meeting, agreed on who had to do what, excused himself and got in his black SUV which doubled up as the village hearse.

When Desfourneaux drove past Minnie's Restaurant, he saw Matthew walking out. He quickly made a U-turn, called out to him and parked on the pavement.

"What's up dude?"

"Sorry Matthew. I did not mean to pounce on you like this, my apologies."

"All good brother, what's cookin?"

"Fiona has bought a meat processing machine which she wants to install on my farm where the chicken coops were. I am going to go there now, but I am going to need your help."

Oh shit, Matthew thought.

99

"What can I do for you brother?"

"We are going to have to clean out that whole space. You know how fastidious Fiona is about cleanliness. And we are going to have to strengthen the floor. There are lots of cracks. That floor was never made for heavy machinery. Oh, god, why did I agree to this? When Fiona talked about buying a machine, I thought it was just big talk. I never thought she would actually do it. Now I have a crisis."

Desfourneaux looked perplexed, then looked up.

"Matthew, do you have spare time and workers to help me? I simply cannot keep up with everything at the moment. I have a funeral for that boy tomorrow afternoon and as you know, I have to do my rounds at the old age home tonight. Can you help me?"

"Sure bro. No sweat. We will fix that place for you. You mean that big building where you had all the chicken runs? That place is a complete mess. Where are all the chickens now?"

"Most of them died. I only have a few free-range chickens left. The butcher will take them next week."

"And what about the freezer?" Matthew asked.

"Oh, I switched it off this morning. I don't use it now that I don't have chickens left. I also let the staff go until I can sort things out again. With the government's approval of imported chicken meat, there is not much of a market left. Chicken farming is no longer profitable. That's why I switched it off – it was using far too much power."

Oh shit, Matthew thought.

"Desfourneaux, Desfourneaux! Quick! Help!" It was Minnie. "Quick, get a doctor, quick!" She tore her apron off and ran back into the restaurant. It was obvious that there was no time for questions or answers.

Desfourneaux called Dr Riaan's surgery. "We have an emergency at Minnie's restaurant. Please doctor, can you come here as quickly as possible? It is a life or death situation. Please! Immediately! Not? Then send the ambulance. Where is it? Excellent! Thank you, thank you."

Within a minute or two they could hear the siren as the ambulance approached. Minnie appeared in the door again.

"Is that the ambulance?"

"Yes," Desfourneaux said, "the ambulance is only a block away. They had it on standby at the roadblock on the freeway. Dr Riaan said it would be quicker if the ambulance took the patient to the doctor's surgery."

The ambulance came to a halt in front of the restaurant. Two paramedics ran into the building. After a couple of minutes, one returned to fetch a bottle of oxygen and a gurney from the rear of the ambulance and disappeared back into the restaurant.

Desfourneaux and Matthew peered through the front windows. They could see people on their knees amongst the tables but not much more.

"I wonder what is going on." Matthew said.

By then people started to gather in front of the restaurant, all wanting to know what had happened and why the ambulance was parked there. Some of them also looked through the windows, listened to the voices in the restaurant, but nobody could work out what was going on.

After about twenty minutes, the paramedics emerged with someone, covered with a bright red blanket, on the stretcher. One had a drip bag in his hand which he held high above his head. They loaded their passenger into the ambulance, slammed the back door closed and disappeared down the road with the siren on full volume.

It was only when they were completely out of sight that everybody heard the sobbing. It was Minnie. She stood at the entrance of the restaurant with a napkin over her face.

Desfourneaux walked up to her and took her hand. "What happened, sweet child?"

"It was one of the old ladies from the Methodist Church. She came here for breakfast as usual. Soon after I put her usual coffee with cold milk and one sugar on the table, she started to cough. I thought she burnt herself, but then she said she had a terrible pain in her chest and fell on the ground. The paramedics thought she may have had a heart attack... I feel so terrible, I don't even know her name." She buried her face in the napkin again.

"Please take care of this. I have to get to the doctor." Desfourneaux handed Minnie over to Matthew, got in his vehicle and disappeared down the road.

It was nothing less than ominous that the hearse was in hot pursuit of the ambulance.

Dr Riaan's surgery and clinic were on the northern side of the village, on the edge of the forest. Its high elevation gave the property an incredible view to the south, over the entire village and the freeway that curled into the forest. In the distance one could see the mountains that surrounded the village with a rocky embrace. During the early mornings and at sunset, the doctor and his patients were treated to the most remarkable displays of colour, especially when the clouds rolled off the mountains to dance in the sky. Many years ago, when he bought that stretch of land, the doctor was attracted to the ancient trees that created an enormous canopy over a large section of the property. He first built a house with a surgery and later added a small clinic where he could handle emergencies and stabilisations before the patients could be transferred to larger, better equipped and staffed hospitals. He also had a dispensary from where he provided the local community with medicines and typical seasonal medical care, like flu and hay fever. It was a goldmine. The old age home provided him with a steady stream of patients that had every ailment from dermatitis to dementia and the forest workers occasionally ended up at the surgery with broken bones, cuts and snake bites.

In the end, Dr Riaan became a very wealthy man that liked to travel abroad every so often, bought clothing overseas and drove an expensive car which he replaced, like clockwork, every year. There were rumours that the doctor, who was also known to dress in slightly flamboyant clothing, that was always a touch too tight fitting, paid special attention to his younger male patients in preference to the rest. Nevertheless, he was well loved and respected by all.

When the ambulance roared up the road, Dr Riaan appeared at the front door of his clinic. He no longer had a full head of hair, but what remained was cut with a shaved parting and longer hair brushed to the side. He wore a snug-fit purple silk shirt, beige pants, purple suede sharp-toed slip-on shoes and a matching pair of purple funky frame reading glasses – a look which he copied from the Italian men's fashion magazine, L'Uomo, which was on the coffee table of his reception area. He looked expensively dressed, but just a tad awkward and hemmed in.

The paramedics parked the ambulance in front of the clinic entrance, then hopped out and rolled the gurney, with the patient still strapped in position, out of the rear of the vehicle.

"What is the matter with the patient?" Dr Riaan asked.

"Possible cardiac failure. We did an ECG on the way here. She had chest pain and arrhythmia. We gave her Aspirin and Nitro-glycerine when we picked her up. She is lucid and a little more stable now doctor."

"Great. Bring her in. Can you help me? I don't have a nurse today. Let's get some blood from her. I need to see if she has any enzymes in her blood."

Dr Riaan looked at the terrified face of the old lady who stared at him from behind the oxygen mask and said: "Good morning ma'am. How are you feeling? Are you ok? What is your name?"

"Mary Rose" she said.

"Mary Rose? What a nice name. Wasn't there a ship named after you?" He smiled at her, which made her feel a little at ease.

"Hehe doctor. It was the other way around. "

The clinic looked like an art gallery. Dr Riaan had a great love for paintings and drawings which ensconced every inch of the walls in the building. Long, sumptuous curtains covered the windows which made the emergency room feel homely and peaceful.

The men expertly lifted the patient off the gurney and on to the closest bed. Within seconds, Dr Riaan attached a few sticky plasters with electrodes to Mary's chest that powered up the graphics on the ECG monitor. As soon as that was done, he took a vile of blood and put it into a machine for analysis. He listened to her heart, lungs and tested for oedema on the lower parts of her legs.

Once he had a reasonable understanding of her medical profile, he explained to Mary: "I am afraid you had a heart attack earlier. I can see that by the presence of enzymes in your blood. Your ECG also shows a couple of irregularities. Don't worry, I think you are ok for the moment. The best I can do is to get you as stable as possible, but then we have to get you to a proper hospital where you can get specialist care."

"Thank you doctor," Mary said. She timidly reached out to touch his hand.

"Ok, I'm going to leave your drip in place. I also injected some additional medication into the bag. Once it is empty, I think we can start preparing you for the ambulance journey to the city."

"Thank you doctor," she said again and squeezed his hand.

Dr Riaan then offered the paramedics a cup of tea. As they prepared to leave the room, Desfourneaux appeared at the entrance.

"Doctor, my apologies for arriving unannounced. May I …" And indicated that he wanted to talk to the patient.

"Yes, but keep it short. She needs to rest after her incident," Dr Riaan said, "We'll be back in a minute."

The moment the doctor and the paramedics left the room, Desfourneaux was on his knees next to the bed.

"Mary, my darling Rose, I'm so upset that you are not well."

"I feel better now," Mary said from behind the oxygen mask.

"I heard the doctor said you had a heart attack. I'm so sorry."

He got up and dragged a chair to the edge of the bed, then put both of his hands around hers.

"Mary, my beautiful Rose, I want to put your mind at ease. I am here for you. While you are not well, I'll take care of everything for you. Is there anything you want me to do for you?"

"Please feed Percy, my cat." She could barely get the words out from behind the oxygen mask.

"With pleasure my sweetest Rose. Is there anything else? I'm sure there will be payments to be made for your rent at the home and the doctor …"

"Yes, please."

"For that I will need a Power of Attorney form to take to the bank. Luckily I have one here in my bag. Will you sign it for me then I'll make sure that all your affairs are taken care of while you are getting better?"

He quickly opened his bag, took out a form which he completed in the car earlier, placed it on a tea tray and handed Mary a pen.

"Mr Desfourneaux, you are such a kind man. I don't know what I would have done without you."

"It is with the greatest of pleasure that I will do it for you, my dearest Rose. Do you have any family I should advise?"

"No, Mr Desfourneaux, my sister died last year."

"Then will you sign this document for me, dearest angel Rose?"

She lifted her head to see where the signature needed to go and neatly wrote her name. Mary Rose. At that moment the doctor and the paramedics walked back into the room. Desfourneaux asked them to sign as witnesses, which they did without asking a question. When he put the signed document in his bag, there was a little smile on his face that revealed his two yellow buck teeth - for just a moment.

"Thank you for your trust my Rose blossom," he said to the hapless woman. "Now get better so you and kitty can share your bed again. Remember there is nothing in the world to worry about." He kissed her on the forehead and turned towards the door. "Good day gentlemen." He clicked his heels and left.

"Was that a Power of Attorney we just witnessed doctor?" one of the paramedics asked the doctor.

"Yes, it was."

"I heard that he got Mrs Green to also sign a Power of Attorney when she got sick. When she came out of the hospital, he had taken all her money. There was nothing she could do about it. It may be just a story; I don't know..." The paramedic laughed and had a sip of his tea.

"No, I heard similar stories of other old ladies that fell under his spell. He is apparently a very smooth operating conman."

Behind them, the patient's eyes grew bigger and bigger as she listened to their conversation. She tried to speak, but only little grunt noises came out of her mouth.

A minute or so later the ECG machine sounded an alarm. Rose had a massive heart attack.

The doctor and the paramedics tried their best to resuscitate her, but nothing helped. She was gone. Later, when they prepared her for cremation, they found a pen still clutched in her hand.

Dr Riaan phoned Desfourneaux to tell him the bad news. He was at Minnie's coffee shop, in search of Matthew. When Desfourneaux told Minnie, she broke down and cried for an hour.

I heard about the news when Matthew stormed into my cottage.

"What's wrong Matthew!"

"Bro, there is big shit. We are gonna have to get Cindy or Candy or whatever her name was out the fridge at Cheerio. It's that boy's funeral tomorrow and to crown it all, that old geezer switched the freezer off. She is going to go off if we don't do something."

"What are we going to do?"

"I have no idea bro, but we are gonna have to do something in a heartbeat, before that old bastard or Fiona go to the farm.

"Come bro, get your shit so we can go. We don't have time."

I grabbed whatever I thought necessary and followed Matthew to his truck. My long weekend from the city turned into a very long nightmare.

On the way to Cheerio, we drove past Minnie's restaurant. Desfourneaux saw us and indicated that we should stop.

"Yo, what's up now dude? We are going to sort out that chicken shit for you." Matthew clearly struggled to hide his irritation.

"Our sister, Mary Rose from the Methodist Church sadly passed away an hour ago," Desfourneaux said in his funeral director voice. "May she rest in peace."

"Oh fuck, not another one." Matthew said.

"Yes, she is in the arms of the angels now, looking down upon us with eternal love."

"Christ Desfourneaux, get a grip. You're talking to me, Matthew! What am I supposed to do about it? Must I bring beers when I get back?"

"There is no need to get aggressive during a time of mourning son. You can do me a favour when you are out there, if you are inclined to do so. Our sister Mary Rose elected to be cremated. Please will you look for me if there is enough gas at our little crematorium?"

"With pleasure, I will let you know when I get back."

As we drove off, Matthew leaned across to me and laughed.

"Our asses are saved bro. Today was our lucky day!"

We light cigarettes and turned up the radio. Armin van Buuren was playing "Another You." The day turned out better than I expected.

Chapter 7

A New Beginning

Like all country towns, this one was also built around a main road that roughly cut the village in half. All the business activities were neatly arranged next to one another, from the Spit and Polish on the one end to Fiona's little complex on the other end. In between were a few restaurants, including Minnie's Waffle and Deli, the hardware store, the supermarket and the museum. Right in the centre was the village square, but unlike other country towns, there was no church that dominated the square. (The church was built next to the school on the northern side of the village.) Instead, it was overlooked by Minnie's Waffle and Deli, the police station, the forest and the chapel which belonged to Desfourneaux's funeral parlour.

The chapel was used by all denominations for weddings and funerals, which meant that it generated a good, steady income for Mr Desfourneaux. The chapel was built by Trudi's late husband and was primarily constructed out of wood from the local forests. It was a masterpiece. The design principle was simple, imaginative and brilliant. The floor plan was a perfect square. Enormous beams reached from the four corners of the base of the building to the crest of the roof where they met. Walls built with cut local sandstone and stained glass windows, depicting the local forests and

115

plants, filled the void between the beams, which gave the building a natural gothic feel. Floors, crafted from the same sandstone, formed a dramatic offset against the dark wooden doors, seating and podium made by the famous Van der Merwe Joinery.

The story of the chapel was told in the museum on the upper end of the main street. Apparently the beams were carefully selected and cut in square lengths before they were dried under heavy weights to retain their shape. Once dried, they were re-cut and taken to the river where they were soaked for a month. Once they were sufficiently wet, they were again weighed down and dried to create the perfect arches needed for the chapel roof. Only once they were sufficiently dry, were they machined and installed. The result was breath-taking.

Desfourneaux paid cash for the work. Nobody was sure where he got the money from, but there was general consensus that he sweet-talked the money out of numerous people that came to live in the old-age home and died there over the years. The story of the village, however, started much earlier when copper was discovered in the vicinity. The mining activities soon ended and business activities graduated to forestry, milling and strangely enough, stargazing. At the turn of the previous century, Oxford University sent a couple of cosmologists to the area to look for a suitable place to build an observatory. They acquired a piece of land on

Mount Pushover and built the basic structures of an observatory but never completed the work because the world was plunged into war in 1918. The money ran out and they returned to England. Fiona eventually acquired that stretch of land which made her the biggest land owner in the area.

There was not much else to see in the museum, apart from a few old pictures and tools that were donated by the locals.

The first target for improvement, that also promised to generate immediate income, was the village square. On the very next day, after the planning meeting at the Spit and Polish, a bulldozer was seen levelling the ground on the square. The soil was aerated and fresh rolls of instant lawn was installed across the entire area. Finally, walkways were created with large square stepping stones along the outer edges of the square. A week later, a number of white canvass canopies arrived, which were ingeniously suspended with steel cables from four massive beams that were erected to straddle the square and at the same time mimicked the shape of the chapel. A clever cradle, suspended from the beams, contained space for projection equipment and laser lights. The canvass surrounded by the oak trees that were planted about a hundred years earlier, created a cosy, attractive area where one could host a variety of events. The people at the mill donated an entire collapsible floor for the square which they kept in a neat stack at their storage area. To round it off, special low energy solar lights were installed to create a romantic mood on the square and all along the walkways in the forest across the road. Needless to say that the old bright street lights were moved to another part of the village. When it was done, the new lights, with the illuminated chapel as a backdrop, looked magical at night – the ideal romantic getaway to meet many new people and perhaps a new love.

All that was missing was food and music – and people. To make sure that the people would come, Matthew called upon the help of his graphic designer friend, Brendan. Matthew found him on a yacht in the Mediterranean Sea and convinced him to create a comprehensive marketing identity, with brochures that would entice and solicit business for the village and surroundings. When the material was delivered, it included a brand new village identity, a logo, advertising material for magazines and the internet, animated GIFs for social media, and new signage that could be used to attract more visitors from the freeway. He even went so far to recommend concepts for video material that could be shot with drones in the surrounding areas.

But I'm getting ahead of myself. Before we could welcome people in the village, Matthew and I had to take care of important business at the Cheerio chicken farm. We arrived there shortly after midday. One could see at a glance that the dilapidated place was in urgent need of improvement. The entrance to the farm was somehow incongruous with the rest of the surroundings. Two beautifully designed walls in the Cape Dutch style, complete with two gigantic urns, flanked an enormous steel gate that was open and which hung precariously on its bottom hinge.

 Many years of wind, rain and dust left their mark on the paint-work that almost matched the colour of the dirt road that led to the estate. The road extended past a lane of old poplar trees, presumably planted by a caring previous owner. When we drove past the lane, we reached a sharp turn to the right that led to a clearing in the woods. Immediately on the left was the warehouse, which I recognized from our previous nocturnal visit. Next to the warehouse, recessed towards the back was the refrigeration unit, which was the same brown white colour as the entrance. Littered everywhere around the buildings was old farm equipment, machinery, hardware and building material. Some of those things must have been there for a very long time because saplings and creepers grew out of the soil that amassed in the crevices between the piles of things that were stacked everywhere.

Straight ahead were the remains of a house, vandalised and apparently occupied by vagabonds. Around the house was a chicken wire fence with a little garden gate.

Matthew parked his truck in front of the house.

"Let's see who is here. We don't want visitors to check in on us."

A ginger cat appeared in a doorway and ran towards us. He stopped at the garden gate, stood up, rubbed his face against the wires and talked to us. A sucker for animals, I made friends with the cat and was tempted to take him home.

"This is weird. There must be people living here."

"I agree. Look how tame and well fed the cat is...."

Matthew walked towards the back of the house and called "Hello! Hello!" but there was no reply.

"Looks as if it's all clear. Let's go inside." We got back in the truck to move it closer to the warehouse. Just as well - as I closed my door, an enormous dog appeared from the back of the building. It was one of those dogs that had a big slobbering mouth with spit that flew all over the place. The dog jumped up against my side of the truck, barking and growling and spitting all over the window. It was disgusting, looked rabid and vicious.

"Let's get out of here!" I shouted at Matthew.

He threw the truck in gear and put his foot on the accelerator. The wheels spun and made a huge dust cloud which must have frightened the dog. We drove to the warehouse and parked right in front of the door.

"Damn, that was close! That creature would have bitten us. Does it belong to Desfourneaux?" I asked.

"I dunno."

We looked towards the house but could not see the dog.

"C'mon bro, let's get going. We better be quick, we don't have much time."

We opened the sliding door, which brought eerie memories back from the previous night we were there. Tiny streaks of sunlight streamed through millions of little rust holes in the old corrugated roof.

"This is where Fiona wants her polony machine installed." I followed Mathew into the cavernous space. "All of this disgusting chicken shit must come out. Damn! It stinks! Look at this, and there are heaps and heaps of it outside too. That stupid hoarding penny pinching Desfourneaux never realised that he could sell it as fertilizer."

"I have a plan," I said. "Let's call the local fertilizer suppliers and tell them they can have all this crap for free, provided they take everything away and clean it out. That will save us an enormous amount of work."

"Sweet my brother. That will work!" Matthew smiled his lapdog smile at me. He made me laugh. I used my phone to Google the fertilizer companies in the area and called the closest one. When I explained the proposition, it was a no-brainer. They could start shovelling the shit away the next day.

"It's a shame we are going to have to fix the roof. I love the way the sunlight shines like lasers through the holes," I said.

"You are giving me an idea. Perhaps we should have a party here before the roof is fixed. We can put lights on top of the roof and put a smoke machine inside. It'll look awesome! Let's do it bro, it'll be super awesome."

"Yeah, but we might be in the slammer before we can organise that if we don't sort out that damn woman in the fridge," I said. I started to shiver as I felt panic brewing in my stomach.

"Ok brother, let's look around and find the best alternative."

At the back of the warehouse, we found a door that opened to the rear of the property. It was revolting. Heaps of chicken shit covered the entire clearing in the forest. What a waste I thought, it was such a pretty place and yet Desfourneaux and his workers befouled it with this unspeakable mess. There was no question about it. We had to have the space cleaned up if we wanted to have a party or if we wanted to make a success of the kibble business.

I refused to walk any further and suggested that we look elsewhere. Fortunately we did not have to look very far.

Nestled between the trees, well removed from the rest of the buildings, we found an old family cemetery. It was obvious that the place had not been visited in a long time. It was covered in a thick layer of leaves and indigenous ground cover that effectively hid the tombstones from view. Only a few crosses, covered in green and white lichens, some with inscriptions and others not, found their way through the growth. We could not believe our luck when we saw that one of the graves had collapsed and left a huge gaping cavity below the gravestone.

"This is perfect bro," Matthew whispered to me. "Let's do it and get it over with."

We silently walked all the way back to the warehouse and went to the freezer. My heart pounded and I wanted to hurl. Having to deal with this - stone cold sober - was a very different thing from having brought her here when we were completely out of it.

Matthew opened the freezer, which was no longer ice cold, but damp and humid inside.

"How are we going to get her out of here Matt? We will not be able to take the trolley through the woods."

"Bro, I think I saw a ladder inside. Let's roll her on the ladder. It will be easier to carry her that way."

"Yes, I certainly don't want to see or touch her." I wanted to cry. I had nothing to do with this mess but I

123

was implicated and complicit in a bloody horrendous situation which had no possibility of a positive outcome.

"Ok, get the ladder. I want to get out of here."

Matthew disappeared into the warehouse and returned with a ladder a minute later. We went to the corner in the back of the freezer and removed the cardboard boxes stacked on the shelves. I was relieved to see that she was still there. What was I thinking? Why would she not be there after all? But what if we were caught red-handed? How the fuck would we explain our way out of this one?

"Matthew, I cannot do this. Look at me! I'm wetter than a porn star's tits with sweat!"

"Don't be such a girl dude. We don't have an option. We have one chance and it is now."

"I'm going to be sick."

"For goodness's sake bro, this will only take a few minutes and then it will be over. C'mon, don't think of what you are about to do. Just help me. Once it's done, it's done. And don't bash the boxes around. You know there is another body next to her!"

We carefully picked Candy off the shelf. I made absolutely certain that I held on to the blankets tightly so that she could not roll out and I had to look at her face. What if her eyes were still open?

We somehow managed to get her on the ladder and Matthew tied her down with a couple of ropes.

We struggled to get her out of the fridge and had to negotiate our way from between the shelving until we reached the freezer door. When we reached the door, Matthew put his end down, opened the door and found a brick which he used as a door stop. From there, we managed to walk easily and without a problem through the warehouse and out of the back door.

"Let's put her down for a moment, I'll close the freezer door, just in case someone arrives here."

The moment Matthew turned his back, the damn dog that attacked me earlier, came charging around the corner. I heard it running towards me, making snorting and gargling noises as it breathed. I froze on the spot. When the thing leaped straight for my face, I could see its eyes, teeth and mouth approaching me in slow motion. The next thing I knew; I was on the floor in the warehouse. Matthew grabbed my hand, yanked me into the warehouse and slammed the door shut. The dog was on the other side, still barking savagely.

"What the fuuuuuuck!"

During the commotion, I fell and hurt my elbow. Blood streamed down my arm.

"I'm going to kill that dog!"

"We are going to have to get you to a doctor. You fell straight into the chicken shit. You will get infection if it is not cleaned right away."

"I think so too. It burns like hell. Thank you, you got me just in time, but what are we going to do Matt? It sounds as if that crazy dog is pulling the blankets off Candy."

"Oh, there you are!" The female voice came from the other side of the warehouse.

"I saw your truck and I looked everywhere for you Matthew." She walked towards us.

He looked at me and said: "Now we are fucked bro, double fucked."

"Hi Fiona," I said. "What are you doing here?"

"I came to see what progress was made with this place, because the machine will be delivered soon. Oh, my poor boy! What happened to your arm?"

I explained that I slipped and fell when I tried to get away from the dog that was outside.

"We are going to have to get him to a doctor Fiona. I'm scared Max will get an infection. This chicken shit is not cool."

"Ok, I'll take him quickly. Will you follow us to the doctor?"

Fiona had a motherly side which I had never seen before.

"I will be in touch. I just need to lock up first."

At the car, Fiona gave me a few wet wipes to clean my arm. It was obvious that she was terrified of getting in contact with my blood. When I managed to get the bleeding under control and most of the blood off my arm, she gave me a towel to wrap around the wound.

On the way to the doctor I told her about my plan to get the fertilizer manufacturers to clean up the place in return for the chicken shit. We also talked about the roof. I suggested that we put a new corrugated iron roof on top of the old one. Matthew already had plans for the resurfacing of the floor. It could happen immediately after the place was cleaned. Fiona was impressed with the ideas and asked me to go ahead the next day. She called the fertilizer suppliers from the car and struck a deal with them.

Dr Riaan was very helpful. He cleaned the wound with peroxide that bubbled all the shit out of the cut. When I cried out in pain, he reassuringly put his hand on my lap and explained that it was almost all over.

In the meantime, Fiona paged through the L'Uomo magazine in the reception area. She was amazed by the Italian models dressed in fabulous formal pants and brogue leather shoes with no visible socks. A while later we left. Me with a bandage around my elbow and Fiona with new ideas in her head.

127

"I need a drink Fiona," I said.

"Ok, let's go to the pub. I have a lot of catch-up to do with a few people. Have you seen Troy by any chance? I'm curious about how my lions are doing?"

"No, I'm afraid I have not seen him. Things have been hectic this side."

I reached into my pants for my phone.

I typed a text message for Matthew. "How are things on your side?"

The reply came almost immediately. "Not to worry, I put the baby to rest."

"Yay. I'm done at the doctor. Fiona is taking me for a drink at the pub. See you there."

"Sweet. See you in a mo."

There were a few regulars at the Spit and Polish. Fiona parked her Land Rover in the bay closest to the entrance. We got out and were welcomed by the breasts. By the time we sat down, our drinks arrived. Fiona's drink had an umbrella, as usual and I got a Viper in support of my friend who was about to arrive.

"I'm so happy," Fiona said. "I went to this revolting, filthy place in Jet Park where I went to look at a meat crusher machine. Well, you have never seen such an untidy, badly managed establishment. No wonder that their polony was infested with that monstrous listeria disease. I felt as if I was on a reality TV show in a room filled with creepy crawlies. Uhg! I am itching all over again just thinking of it. Anyway, I quickly had a look at the machine and made them a ludicrous offer. On my way here, that revolting Mr Gupta called me to say that they accepted my offer. While he was talking to me on the phone I could see him wiping that ugly pock-marked face of his with a MacDonald's napkin. Ugh! How disgusting!"

She took a cigarette out of her purse. "Would you like one?" She asked.

"No thank you," I said.

"Hello." Matthew grinned at us when he walked into the room. He went to stand behind Fiona and gave me his lapdog smile to let me know everything was ok.

"I don't think I'm going to stay for a drink right now. I am covered in chicken shit. Max, would you mind if I have a shower at your place?"

"Not at all, here are my keys."

On his way out Desfourneaux walked in. "Afternoon Matthew. Were you at the farm?"

"Afternoon bro," he said. "Yes, I was. I checked for gas and found six sealed bottles."

"Thank you Matthew. That will be good enough."

Matthew excused himself and left.

"*Bonjour* Fiona ... Max."

"Hello Jan'ee," Fiona replied.

"So what do you think of the improvements in the square?" He asked.

"It looks fabulous. I love it. Tomorrow the two girls from Ginger Cat Linen will be here to help all the accommodation owners. They supply the major hotels. You will see, they have superb quality heavy duty linen, which we can have at corporate rates."

"Will you excuse me please? I also need a bath after the disaster at the chicken farm."

"What disaster was that?" Desfourneaux wanted to know.

"That stupid dog of yours attacked him! When he tried to get away, he fell on his arm. I had to take him to the doctor. You are going to have to do something about that dog!" Fiona put Desfourneaux on the defence.

"My sincere apologies Matt," Desfourneaux said in his funeral director voice.

"Oh, by the way, we arranged with the fertilizer company in the valley to fetch all that chicken shit and clean up that warehouse tomorrow. I hope you don't have a problem with that. Jan'ee, what is the matter with you?

How can you live and work like that? That place is worse than a chicken coop, it is a pig sty! This is your chance to create some order on that farm."

When Desfourneaux tried to say something, she waved her finger in his face and said: "No, no, no. It is arranged. I don't want to hear another word out of your mouth."

I was pleased to go to my cottage. This place became much too hectic for me. It was time to get back to the city. Dealing with taxis and beggars at every intersection seemed surprisingly attractive. I could go to cinema nouveau to watch the latest movies and eat a bucket of popcorn on my own. My car would wait for me in the basement and I would drive back home through the slums, all the way to my little house on the hill that overlooks the street lights, shopping centres and houses in the valley. I would disarm the alarm system, unlock the garage, park my car, then lock my car, lock the garage and re-engage the alarm system. I would then disarm the house alarm, walk past the security beams, unlock the house and open the door to my cocoon. Once inside, I would lock the door behind me, activate the beams around the house and enjoy my privacy.

It occurred to me that to be free in the city, I had to be imprisoned. It was different here. There was a natural freedom that allowed me to be unencumbered by the baggage that came with city life.

Matthew sat outside having a smoke when I arrived.

"May I join you?" I asked.

"Yes, please do." He offered me a cigarette.

I lit the cigarette behind my hand and looked up at him. "So what did you do?"

"It was much easier than I expected bro. I went back inside the warehouse with a stick. The dog was still outside making a hell of a noise, so I just opened the door. At first the dog just stood there and barked, but then I taunted it with the stick until it ran into the warehouse. As soon as it was inside, I slipped outside and closed the door behind me."

"I don't know if that was clever or brave." I said.

"Ha! It was brave!" We both laughed.

"I then checked the place out again and found a wheelbarrow, so I put her into the wheelbarrow and took her to the cemetery. It was quite easy. It was lucky she was not a fat chick, otherwise I would have struggled on my own. I kept her wrapped in the blankets and I'm afraid it was easiest to put her face first into the hole. She slid in there quite easily, but I had a problem getting her feet in all the way, so I put a few stones all around her feet, just in case the dog decided to chow on her."

The thought made me want to vomit.

"Thanks Matt. Where is the dog now?"

"It's still in the warehouse. I thought it best to leave it locked up there for the night. We can let it out tomorrow."

"I'm so tired of all this crap. Let's get something to eat and get some rest. I've had enough of one day. Tomorrow is going to be a huge day."

I went inside, took my clothes off and showered as well as possible with the bandage on my arm. The fresh smell of the body wash replaced the ghastly smell of the chicken coop. It was all good and well shoving most of that girl under a tomb stone, but what if she started to decompose? I saw on the Crime Channel that human bodies smelled terrible when they rot. The smell would have been disguised if the chicken shit remained on the farm, but if it was going to be cleaned - then everybody will be able smell a dead body. Shit.

After I finished cleaning myself, I put fresh clothes on and slipped into my slops. Meanwhile, Matthew was outside, and fiddled about with his phone.

"I don't feel like the pub Matt. Let's go to the supermarket and get some food. It will be nice if we could have some quiet time and talk things through."

"That's a great idea brother. Let's have a chop and 'dop' tonight. It will be super cool."

Later that evening, after a few beers, I said to him: "Matt, we are in trouble. That body is going to start decomposing in a few days and she is going to stink to high heaven. We have no choice; we are going to have to make another plan. I already have another plan. It's risky, but it is the best option."

And that is how it happened that Matthew and I concocted a survival plan to save our asses.

Chapter 8

The Machine

There was genuine sadness the day the whole village came together to say goodbye to Mary Rose. People came from all over the country. From early that morning, cars poured into the village. By ten in the morning all the parking bays around the square were taken and so was every seat at Minnie's Waffle and Deli.

Some of the guest lodges and cottages were in the process of being renovated and the linen from Ginger Cat was still on backorder, so unfortunately many of those places lost out on a golden opportunity to make some money. The people who were finished with renovations reported later at a village gathering that they were able to increase their prices and that the patrons happily paid up to twice as much as the normal rate – and expressed a desire to come back for a more peaceful weekend.

Minnie and her staff worked like slaves. On the night before the funeral, Minnie contacted some of her old staff and asked them to help out on the day. Most of them were very obliging and came to work at dawn to be ready and prepared for the influx of people. Only one disgruntled idiot that everybody hated in any case told Minnie to go fuck herself. The rest soon got back into the swing of things and worked like an old team together. In a way Minnie was truly grateful to Mary Rose. Halfway through breakfast she went to stand in

137

the back door of the restaurant, next to the rubbish bins, put her hands together and said a quick prayer of thank you for the business. Things had been hard lately and she suffered so badly from reflux as a result of all the stress and this would make things just a little bit easier. She rubbed a tear that rolled down her cheek away before she went back with a broad smile, welcomed another table of patrons and said: "Good morning. Thank you for visiting us today. What can I get you?"

The visitors loved Minnie. She epitomised a hard-working mom who cleverly used old family favourites to her best advantage. A few years ago, when she paged through her late mother's recipe book, she found a waffle recipe and things grew from there. She started her little restaurant with next to nothing. She only had enough money to buy a really good coffee machine and an industrial waffle machine apart from the bare necessities for the kitchen. She made all the table cloths and napkins out of plain white fabric with her Elna sewing machine while the children did their homework.

In the weeks before the shop opened and she realised that there was not enough money left for crockery, she opened her display cabinet and took her Noritake dinner service out. It did not have any value sitting in the cupboard. Anyway, she did not really have visitors after that rubbish of a husband beat her up and then dumped her and the children like trash. She sat cross legged in front of the cabinet and put the pieces into a box, one by one, touching and feeling everyone for chips or cracks. She knew there were none, but she checked anyway. It was her wedding present from her parents. She cried as she closed the empty cupboard. Perhaps, yes, perhaps there would be one good thing that would come out of that horrible marriage.

During the first few weeks of trading, she prayed that no more than twelve people would come in at once. She also put her staff on express wash duty so that all the crockery could be recycled and optimised as people came in and out. As part of their employment contract, the staff had to commit an oath, punishable by torturous death, that they would not chip or break anything. And, surprisingly enough, they stuck to that commitment. Eventually, when Minnie could afford more appropriate crockery, she took the Noritake out of service and created a brand new display on the rear wall of the restaurant section – just as a reminder of where they came from.

Minnie, unlike Fiona, did not have grandiose ideas and did not believe in get rich quick schemes. She resigned herself to the fact that she would work hard for the rest of her life and that she would put a little aside for the day she would be able to take a couple of months off and travel overseas - maybe even go for a patisserie course in France. In the early days, she only made waffles and simple meals which she could put together in her basic little kitchen. The ladies at the old age home enthusiastically agreed to make scones, savoury tarts and cheese cake to be sold at the restaurant. Theoretically speaking, it was a perfect solution, but the products were so inconsistent that Minnie had to stop that arrangement. She blamed the considerable fluctuation in taste on either Alzheimer's or eye sight. After all - at a certain age sugar and salt and flour and baking powder all look remarkably similar. The old ladies were extremely put out by the fact that Minnie no longer wanted to sell their products and rebelled by opening a stall on the square opposite the restaurant on weekends, where they sold their cakes and scones cheaply. The war apparently did not last very long. In the end quality prevailed.

The service was scheduled for 11 a.m. The village folk came from all over. They mostly walked to the chapel in little groups, but there were also couples and singles and even a few in wheelchairs. Since Mary belonged to the Methodist faith, the pulpit was covered with a crimson red cloth and a gold cross. A similar larger cloth with the same insignia was draped over the coffin which was positioned in front of the pulpit.

Desfourneaux used a fancy, locally made pine coffin which was stained in a rich dark colour. What nobody knew was that it was a reusable coffin with a collapsible bottom that allowed the cremators to easily position and release the body into a cardboard box during preparation for the furnace. The ladies from the old age home picked armfuls of wild arum lilies at the waterfall which they placed in simple arrangements on and around the coffin. Shortly before eleven the clouds parted and allowed the sun to shine unencumbered through the stained glass. It was a beautiful sight. The Methodist pastor entered through a back door, walked to the sound system, slid a CD into the tray and pressed 'play'. Sombre choral music filled the remaining space while the last people arrived for the ceremony.

I stood quietly at the entrance. Many of the faces that walked past me were familiar even though I did not know them. I saw them at the village hall and the Spit and Polish, where they looked different, and happier in the muted light.

I was so absorbed by everything that was going on around me that I did not notice Matthew sneaking up from behind me.

"Yo, brother. Shall we have a coffee across the road while they send her off to heaven?" He rolled his eyes, making his disdain of the event, with all the associated ritual, abundantly clear.

"Yeah, it's all very sad, but I didn't know the old duck, so there is no point in trying to look as if I care where she is going. Come, Desfourneaux can take care of his own business."

I agreed without saying a word and followed him across the road. Behind us, the doors to the chapel closed when the sermon began.

When we reached Minnie's place, it was empty. The staff frantically cleaned and rearranged tables with fresh tablecloths and flatware. They obviously expected a large turnout for lunch.

We sat down in the open area in front of the restaurant and ordered two skinny cappuccinos.

Before the coffee arrived, Desfourneaux approached us from across the road.

"What do you boys know about gas burners?" He wanted to know. "I cannot get the furnace at the crematorium to work. I don't know how I am going to be able to take care of our dear Mary Rose if I cannot get the fire started!" Sweat dripped from his forehead which he wiped with a large white handkerchief. He was, as usual, dressed in that ghastly oversized black suit - which he probably bought at a charity shop or scavenged after one of the larger men in the community died - with a white shirt and black tie.

"I guess you are going to have to put her in the freezer dude," Matthew responded. "That way you will not have the pressure to get it done immediately."

"You don't understand," Desfourneaux replied breathlessly. "Some of her family want to wait here for her ashes. They expect to get it from me tomorrow morning."

"Ok brother, no sweat." Matthew smiled at the old man. "I will ask Troy for help. He is good with stuff like that. Now go back to the sermon. I'm sure they will need you inside."

I could see how the old man relaxed a little. "Thank you, thank you, that will be wonderful," he said before he walked back to the chapel.

When he reached the other side of the road, Matthew leant across the table and whispered at me: "Now is our chance bro! There is nobody at Cheerio and if we can get Troy to go to the crematorium, the coast will be clear. This is our chance. It is now or never. Call Troy. Quick."

I looked for him amongst my contacts and called.

Troy answered the phone with his happy-go-lucky voice. "Hey brother! What's happening, hey?"

"Hey Troy," I said, "Mr Desfourneaux from the funeral parlour asked if you could please help him at the crematorium. The furnace, for some reason, does not want to fire up. Are you very busy at the Lion Park?"

"No, not at all. There is not much going on here. The lions are ok, but I am running very short of food for them. Sure, I can quickly go there. No sweat my brother."

"Can you go now?"

"Yeah, I'll go there now."

Matthew listened to the conversation and by the time we said our goodbyes, I could see he was ready to leave.

"Let's do it bro, let's get out of here. We are not going to get another chance like this soon," he said, gulped down his coffee and got up.

I burnt myself downing my coffee, messed all over my mouth, which I wiped as gentlemanly as possible, left money on the table and followed Matthew to his truck.

"You will see it will only take a few minutes, bro. We just need to get the wheelbarrow when we get there. We can get in and out of there before anybody has noticed."

When we turned to the Cheerio estate, a terrible smell and a cloud of black dust hung over the buildings.

"Oh, no," I said, "I forgot that the fertilizer people were still working here to clear out all the chicken shit. I think it is their last day here."

"As long as they are busy, we can quickly do our thing." Matthew grinned nervously at me.

We stopped in front of the warehouse. I opened the door briefly to have a look at what was going on inside. Someone with a bobcat scraped the last of the shit out of the warehouse and was loading it on a truck.

Matthew sneaked around the side of the building to get the wheelbarrow. When he came back, he said: "You will not believe what I just saw. Desfourneaux's dog is dead. I saw its body next to the back door."

"It was a fucking hideous dog anyway," I said. "C'mon let's go!"

We walked to the farm cemetery as fast as we could. When we reached the forlorn tombstones, I could see the out of place pile of stones Matthew stacked there.

We removed the stones until the blanket was visible. Candy was, as Matthew explained, shoved head first, under a large slab of granite with a curious inscription.

"Here lies my wife:

Here let her lie!

Now she's at rest

And so am I."

The grieving husband either settled for a discounted arrangement on the burial, or the tombstone installers did a particularly bad job because the grave was severely damaged by erosion. The cavity under the slab was large enough to comfortably accommodate an animal like a warthog, but we were not going to take any chances. Can you imagine what would have happened if she started to decompose or an animal scavenged in there and retrieved human bones? Once the stones were all set aside, we stood at the end of the grave. Without a word, we readied ourselves to pull on those feet that were mercifully still wrapped in blankets. Even though my heart raced, I tried to keep as calm as possible for both our sake and waited for Matthew to give me the signal. When it came, it required hardly any effort to pull Candy out of the hole.

I was surprised to feel how stiff she still was after some time out of the freezer and was extremely grateful that she did not ooze any excrement and other nasty body fluids on the blankets. In the end I did not know what to expect; I saw on the Discovery channel what happened to decomposing bodies at those corpse farms where they study the stages of decomposition, but none of those programmes included frozen bodies. Still, in complete silence, as if we rehearsed it before, we put her in the wheelbarrow, which I have to add, was not designed for the shape of a human body. When we finally managed to get her positioned firmly enough, her ass somehow hooked into the arch of the barrow and her shoulders rested on the rear rim, between the handles. That meant that when Matthew lifted the handles, her face was positioned between his legs. If she was not covered, she would have had a clear view of Nirvana.

Believe you me, if it was not such a risky business, I would have seen the humour in the situation, but instead ran ahead of Matthew to make sure that we would not encounter any unwanted prying eyes. He followed with the body in the wheelbarrow, walking awkwardly with legs astride to make room for her veiled face below his pudenda. When we eventually got to the parking area, we put her on the back of the truck as quickly as possible and covered her again with the garbage that was still on Matthew's truck.

By the time we were done, I don't know who was more freaked out, Matthew or I, but we were both perfect candidates for Fiona's Urbanols.

Matthew made a quick turn and headed to the main road. From there we drove the short distance to Panthera Park. By the time we reached the main entrance, we were both too stressed and terrified to say a word. What if this plan did not work? We were lucky. The place was deserted because everyone was either at the funeral or the crematorium. After the short journey along the dirt road, he stopped in front of the main entrance gate.

"Let me jump out here. I know where Troy keeps the set of emergency keys."

I ran into the canteen area and straight to the framed picture of Elon Musk. Behind the picture was a recess with remote controls and keys. I grabbed them and ran back to the truck. Every second counted. We had to finish our business before Troy came back from the crematory. At the truck, we tried all the remote controls until we eventually found one that opened the first gate.

We moved forward. The gate closed behind us. We then had to find the second remote control. After a number of attempts, we managed to open the second gate. Somehow, when that second gate closed behind us, we both relaxed – for a moment. It was familiar, like when we went on a game drive, looking for the lions relaxing in the shade under the trees. We looked at each other and smiled. Matthew grabbed my leg and said: "It's almost done – we are going to be ok. Troy said that he rationed the food because he was low on kibbles, which means those lions are ravenous. The evidence will be gone in an hour."

We drove around until we could see the lions and parked facing away from them, so that once we disposed of the body, we could simply drive off, to give the lions a clear view of the food we brought for them.

"Ok, bro, it's now or never!" Matthew said.

We got out of the truck and hopped on the back. The two lionesses looked at us but appeared to enjoy the shade under a large tree too much to care.

"I guess we are going to have to get her out of the blankets Matt."

"Yes, otherwise the cats are going to struggle to reach her and we must leave as little evidence as possible."

Once we opened the rear flap of the truck, we lifted the corpse and turned her sideways so that she could freely roll out of the blankets from the edge of the flap. We had one last look at the lions and when it was obvious that they paid no attention to us, we positioned ourselves to let go of the dead woman. I imagined her to be blue and pock marked with decomposition. There were no flies around, and I silently prayed that I would not see maggots coming out of her eyes, but I did not want to look either. Mercifully, she did not smell bad. Regardless of her condition, I knew that lions happily fed on carrion.

"Are you ready brother?" Matthew asked. I could see he was green in the face, even though he tried to look strong.

"If we don't do it now, I'm not going to be able to do it, so c'mon. Are you ready?"

"Yes," I said, "I'm ready."

"Ok, here we go … 1 … 2 … 3!"

When Matthew got to 3, we yanked the free side of the blankets and let the body fall from the truck. It rolled free and hit the ground with a bounce and loud "clunk."

"What the hell?" I shouted. "What was that?"

We peered over the side of the vehicle.

"You asshole!" I yelled at Matthew. "That's not a dead woman! That's the bloody mannequin that was in my room."

I could not believe what I saw.

"Where is the bitch then?"

"I don't know. Didn't you say the door was open when you woke up? She probably left when we were asleep."

My disbelief quickly turned into a huge sense of relief.

And then I laughed. Hysterically.

"Sorry bro. I feel like such an idiot. We were as high as a giraffe's pussy that night. All I could see was a dead woman in the dark. How was I supposed to know there was a mannequin in your room?"

"And now what?" I asked.

Before Matthew could say anything, a vehicle approached much faster than was allowed on the dirt road. There was a loud explosion. I felt my eyes burn before it turned black.

When I woke up in Dr Riaan's surgery, my eyes were on fire.

"Are you crazy?" Troy stood next to me. "What the fuck were you doing? We saw you on the closed-circuit cameras. In fact, the whole fucking world saw you on the CCTV live feed. What did you do, you stupid bastards?"

"What happened?" I asked.

"One of the security guards thought you were poachers and smacked you with teargas," Troy replied. "But what the fuck were you doing in the lion paddock with a mannequin?"

"Where is Matthew?"

"He is ok. He is still out cold."

"It was just a prank Troy. It was a little fun. I'm sorry."

The 'prank' made us world famous within a few hours. The video material, once again, made the YouTube trending list for a few days. Some viewers on the Internet were enraged by our impertinence to disturb the lions and others thought we were the coolest of dudes, leaving a body in the paddock for everyone to get a scare. Just as well that we never revealed the real reason for our visit to the lions. The enraged people sent more donations for better security and the ones that laughed at us sent more donations for pranks. But most importantly, we were off the hook.

The next day Fiona summonsed us to her shop at the top end of the street. After she thoroughly berated us, she thanked us for the money that poured in and demanded that we made sure her machine got properly installed the following week. She arranged for it to have a comprehensive overhaul before the delivery.

"What still needs to be done?"

As usual, she waved her cigarette in the air every time she had a drag. She looked classy and relaxed in a green knee length skirt and a white top. Dangling around her neck was a glass object on a leather string that was probably made by some or other glass craftsman she encountered on one of her frequent journeys abroad. The one thing I really admired about Fiona was that she consistently supported the artists she got to know – no matter if they were well known or not. She bought things from people if she liked the work they did and that was admirable. Perhaps that was also the reason why her shop was stocked with an interesting variety of things that she found or that people brought to her.

Make no mistake, even though she was a tough cookie, she had a kind side. I once checked her out when someone brought her some really awful leather and metal jewellery. She took the items, one by one, out of the box and looked them over while there was a little twitch on the right hand side of her upper lip.

"Honey," she said. "Mmmmmm… interesting … different, I would say." She put the stuff back in the box. "I'm not sure if my clients are ready for this sort of thing." When the wannabe artist whinged and almost begged her to buy the stuff she said: "Perhaps you should consider leaving it here on consignment – then we'll see what happens."

After they agreed on the consignment terms and the artist left in his clapped out rusty old Toyota Tazz, Fiona made sure the box was out of sight. She simply kicked it under a rack of colourful dresses with her pointy half-height heel. A week later the items were rebranded, repackaged and sold as handmade organic tribal jewellery. The foreign visitors could not buy enough of them.

"Max? I asked you a question."

"Oh, sorry Fiona, I will check up on the fertilizer people, but I think they finished yesterday."

"In that case that entire building needs to be washed down and painted. I'm sure we will choke to death on chicken shit dust in that dump of a building. Get the children from the orphanage to do it. It will give them something to do apart from playing with each other!"

"Are you out of your mind Fiona? What the fuck?! We will have to get people in with pressure spray machines to do it." I could not believe that woman sometimes.

"The most important is to get the floor ready. I saw the specifications you sent me and I arranged with the builders to cast a brand new floor on top of the existing one, with re-enforcement."

"And what about the electricity?" Fiona wanted to know.

"Oh, the people from the electricity department were busy with new cables to Cheerio. I'm not sure how far they are with the installation, but I'll ask Mr Desfourneaux."

"Thanks Max, please make sure those lazy bastards do not slip up."

"Sure thing. Come to think of it, where is Mr Desfourneaux?"

"He and Troy are busy fixing the crematorium, which they should have done yesterday when the two of you messed around like adolescents. Anyway he is distraught about that dog of his. Who knows? It probably got poisoned when it ate one of those diseased chickens. It was a revolting dog. He'll get over it. But look who is here. It's Percy. I adopted Mary's cat. Hello Percy. Who is a sweet kitty? Percy, come here my gorgeous darling."

Percy obviously loved the attention and rubbed himself against the leg of Fiona's chair.

"From now on, Percy will be our shop cat - and Max, if he comes to visit you at the cottage, be nice to him!"

"Sure! I love cats." I was sure poor Percy would have died a terrible death if Desfourneaux looked after him.

"Would you like some tea?" Fiona asked.

"Yes please."

"Why are you so quiet Matthew?"

"While you were talking, I was thinking. It is time for us to organise an awesome party. We have all gone through lots of shit and we did some amazing things. We need to have a good time too." Matthew jiggled his chair. The infirm joints of the old wooden frame squeaked every time he moved, which irritated Fiona.

"Yes, you are right. We are almost ready to do our first major visitor campaign. A few people are still dragging their feet with the accommodation, but we will eventually just have get going, regardless if they are ready or not."

Fiona got up to make us some tea.

"By the way Max, you are going to have to move out of your cottage next week. All the other ones have been refurbished. Yours is the only one that still needs to be fixed up."

As she picked up the tray with used cups and saucers to go to the kitchen, there was a thundering explosion that shook the building. She got such a fright that she dropped everything on the floor. Matthew almost fell off the chair he was riding.

It took us a second or two to recover sufficiently to get up and look in the direction of the explosion. All that we could see was a large cloud of smoke in the valley near the Cheerio estate.

"I wonder what the hell that was," Fiona said. "Oh, for god's sake, I hope nobody got hurt. C'mon, let's go and see if everyone is ok on that side of the village. Come with me."

"Bro," Matthew said, "that does not look good. That smoke comes from my side of the village. I seriously hope there wasn't an explosion at the brewery or ... the crematorium!"

I got into the back of the Land Rover behind Matthew. Fiona threw her handbag on his lap. By the time she started the vehicle, there were people everywhere. They came out of the shops, restaurants, the old age home, and the municipal buildings – from everywhere. I never knew there were so many people in the village.

"Get out of the road you tired old bitches!" Fiona shouted at two old ladies, who at the last minute, turned round and waved at us with huge smiles on their faces. Fiona nodded and waved back timidly. "I have no idea how those two knew there was something wrong - they are both as deaf as a doorknob," she muttered. "Get out of my way!" Fortunately, the rest of the people in the street could hear the roaring engine and made way for us.

I was surprised that Fiona did not have some kind of emergency siren in the car – she virtually owned the bloody village. When we got to the T junction at the highway, we turned right towards Cheerio. The cloud of smoke dissipated by then. Surprisingly enough, Fiona was a damn good driver. She weaved through the traffic, through the sharp curves along the pass, occasionally hurling abuse at a slow or stupid driver, but never made me feel endangered for a second. Apart from her cursing, it was quiet in the car. Matthew obviously stressed about the distillery. He made several futile attempts to call his partner which made him even more anxious.

At Cheerio, we could see a large revolving cement truck exiting from the estate. Fiona stopped in front of the vehicle, forcing it to stop. Matthew got out. He had a brief discussion with the driver and got back into the car.

"He said the explosion happened further down the road. All is ok here. They are busy casting the new floor," he said.

As we travelled further down the road, Fiona cried: "Oh no! It's the crematorium. I'm sure it's the crematorium! Shit, shit, shit, I hope Troy is ok!"

Ahead of us we could see a fire truck taking the turnoff to the crematorium. We followed it down the road to the building on Desfourneaux's farm. There was a lot of smoke and one could see people running around, ghostlike, through the haze. The fire truck slammed on brakes next to the building in a cloud of dust that made the visibility even worse.

Fiona stopped at a safe distance under the canopy of an enormous tree and got out. Incredibly, within seconds, there was water spewing out of the fire hoses onto the building. I could see there was a fire in the roof of the building, which was quickly doused. We looked around to see if anybody was injured or needed help, but the few workers we saw earlier looked as if they were in shock, but not injured. The firemen offered to take them to the doctor which they declined.

It was the first time I ever saw a crematorium and was fascinated by the thought that this was the place where many people from the surrounding area finally lost their human form to be returned to nature as dust. I decided to look around the building. It was a hideous looking structure, perfunctory in its design, presumably created for the sole purpose to destroy the physical remains of a person. To my amazement it worked just like a typical factory, with a receiving side, a production facility in the middle and a dispatch side. Wow, I thought, how macabre. One had to be particularly weird to choose cremation as a career or a job. I presumed that was also why there was not much competition in that line of business. Perhaps I was just stupid and uneducated in the business of human disposal and the recycling of possessions? Perhaps there were websites on the dark side of the Internet dedicated to the recruitment of individuals that looked like the grim reaper who aspired to manage facilities like these or to power an entire death industry, manned by lawyers, retirement fund managers, traders in metal implants, antique dealers, funeral parlours and churches that were always starved of money? Perhaps that was where all our belongings ended up at the end of a productive life? Every hair on my body stood upright. Indeed, perhaps and I became increasingly more certain as I thought about it, there were training schools in the shadows that schooled these people in the art of seduction of old and vulnerable people, or in the cultivation of guilt that yielded maximum revenues for the churches, that in return, propelled their members smoothly into eternity, as if smothered in KY jelly, with consoling faces as plastic as the flowers on their coffins. Perhaps there was an entire secret society like the Masons, under our noses, rehearsing their new recruits to speak in convincing tones and enunciations, endowed to them by fallen angels, to extract maximum benefit out of their targets before they finally set fire to their remains.

I vomited. I heaved but nothing much came out, perhaps because I only had a cup of tea with Fiona earlier in the day. The darkness around the building was even more suffocating than the smoke and the soot and the dust.

"Are you ok, buddy?" It was Matthew. "Let's get you some water. Put this over your nose and mouth."

He gave me a hanky and helped me around the building into a room where there were cardboard boxes large enough to contain a human body, stacked to the roof. Streaks of sunlight streamed through the unprotected window, making patterns on the walls and the floor.

"There has to be a toilet somewhere here..." Matthew searched while looking around the boxes. That's how we found Desfourneaux. He sat on a little bench against one of the exterior walls, crouched up like a child with his hands in his artificial hair.

"Mr Desfourneaux?" I said.

"I'm ruined!" he said.

"Are you hurt?"

"No." He looked up at me. His face was covered in soot. So were his hands, his white shirt, bowtie and black suit. He looked so bedraggled that I felt sorry for him.

"Where can I get some water? I need to rinse my mouth. And where is the washroom?"

He pointed in the opposite direction and said: "There – and there is water in the fridge."

Matthew sat on the bench and put his arm around him. "What happened brother?"

"I am not sure. I struggled to get the fire started ... then went outside to check on the gas bottles ... while I was there, everything exploded." Desfourneaux put his face back in his hands. "First the chickens, now this … oh god. *Je suis en merde très profonde.*"

"Excuse me?"

Before Desfourneaux could say anything else, I could hear the click-click of high heel shoes on the cement floor reverberating through the room. "Oh there you are!" Fiona shouted, or, at least, it sounded as if she shouted. "Jannie, are you ok?"

"No, he is seriously rattled," I said, "perhaps we should get him out of here so that he can get himself cleaned up and get something to drink. I am also choked up and want to get out of here." The water helped settle my stomach but I was still nauseous as hell.

"Jannie …" Fiona said, "Can you talk?"

"Yes, Fiona."

"Ok, but let's get out of here first. The firemen can take care of things."

"No, no, no. Mary is in my car. We have to take her back to the fridge at Cheerio."

I could not believe the words that came out of Desfourneaux's mouth.

I thought I would never see the inside of that fridge again after we stored Candy, the bloody mannequin in there, but we duly drove to Cheerio with Desfourneaux, who at that stage looked as if *he* was the one that was retrieved from under a gravestone. This time we relied on a few workers at the construction site to help us carry the coffin via the new side entrance into the refrigeration unit. Needless to say, I could not wait to get out of there. As I walked towards the exit, I noticed the remains of Desfourneaux's dog.

The village and all the shit that happened there, since I arrived a few days earlier, got too hectic for me. I needed to chill. Before we left, we stopped to look at the warehouse renovations. Troy did a fabulous job with the contractors. The warehouse was as clean as a whistle and freshly painted both inside and out. Judging by the thickness of the new cement floor, which was poured on top of the old floor and looked as if it was strong enough to accommodate a fighter plane, the building was ready for Fiona's machine.

Later that evening, I had a drink with Troy, Desfourneaux, Matthew and Fiona. Minnie also showed her face after she finished cashing up next door.

"What happened at the crematorium?" Minnie wanted to know.

Troy in his happy-go-lucky manner was quick to explain that he had just come back from the crematorium with the firemen and that "things were not as bad as everybody thought. It looked as if part of the smoke stack became unstable and fell into the chimney - which caused a blockage. When Mr Desfourneaux lit the furnace, there was a massive increase in pressure and the whole thing blew out of the smoke stack like a ball out of a cannon. That's why there was such a huge plume of fire and smoke. Mr Desfourneaux can count his lucky stars the kiln was not damaged, otherwise it would have cost him a shit load of money to have it fixed."

"My god! Was anybody hurt?" I once saw that look on Minnie's face when Mary keeled over at the waffle shop.

"No, but they all got a serious fright." Troy laughed. Desfourneaux glared at him like a boy that was flattened by the bully at school.

"We all got a damn fright." Fiona added. "Desfourneaux, how is your drink? You need to drink and get a good sleep tonight."

"I'm ok thanks Fiona," he said in a timid slurring voice.

"Troy, how much repair work needs to be done and how long will it take?"

"I don't know Fiona. We have to get the people here who originally installed the furnace. It is an old unit, so I think there is some upgrading to do as well. Some of those strange bricks on the inside of the kiln are no longer in good condition."

"I'm ruined. I'm ruined ..." is all that Desfourneaux could say.

"Oh shut up Jannie! Don't be such a baby. We will get the suppliers here and get them to fix the thing for you. Don't you have any insurance?"

The old man's face brightened up. "Yes, Fiona, now that I'm thinking about it, I do have insurance. I will go through my documents later tonight. Insurance ... I did not think about the insurance ... May I have another beer?" The breasts brought him a Castle Lager.

"Can I arrange for the machine to be delivered Troy? Are you ready?" Fiona was back in her project management mode.

"Yes, Fiona. The floor needs to cure for another two days, then you can have the machine installed. You must make sure they bring the machine with a truck that has an on-board crane otherwise we will never get the thing in there. Fortunately, the warehouse has those big sliding doors ..."

"Ok, I'll organise for it to be delivered."

"Sorry to interrupt your conversation, but I arranged a craft beer festival and a motherfucker of a trans-party for us at the end of next month. That's six weeks from now."

Everyone looked at Matthew.

"Yes," he added, "the first notifications went out today on Facebook, Tinder and Grindr. As soon as I published it, Event Finder found the event and aggregated it to hundreds, if not thousands of Facebook pages. I hope you don't mind, but I added an entrance fee of R850 per person. If people don't pay, they don't come – as simple as that! That way we will keep the riff-raff out and have a really cool weekend of drinking and party and hopefully some shagging too." He laughed loudly. "What do you say? Let's have a Tequila!"

The fact that Matthew went so far to advertise an event, created a sense of urgency to get things done. That evening Fiona made Troy responsible for the installation of 'the machine' and also agreed that he would test the equipment as soon as possible so that she could stop buying Whiskers for the lions. There was not much left to do in terms of renovations at the site. Now that the floor was cast, only the inspection gangway above the machine needed to be installed. The people at Bend-a-Tube, close to the airport, were already making the components according to Troy's specifications. He expected the pipes, connectors and flooring to arrive any day and was convinced that it would only take a day or two to install.

Fiona took it upon herself to make sure that all the accommodation would be refurbished for the occasion. She called the Ginger Cat girls from the Spit and Polish that evening to demand that all the linen be delivered in good time. In the meantime, the cottages were repainted, the beds were replaced and those horrible

Perspex showers were replaced with stone floors, massage jets and huge glass doors. The Darth Vader fireplaces remained, but they were cleaned out to make sure that they worked efficiently. Percy loved running around while the workers pulled out the old dusty carpets and replaced them with fresh soft carpets that made one's feet feel as if they were massaged when you walked on them. Fiona was adamant that one should want to walk barefoot in the cottages. Even though the rooms were not gigantic, that they should be luxurious, cosy, quaint and memorable. When Fiona saw the first completed cottage, she was almost in tears. "This looks so beautiful ... [sniff, sniff] ... I could retire in an apartment like this," she said and stroked Percy who inspected the interiors with her. "Percy, my darling, I just love the fact that there are no televisions here. If people want to watch the news or whatever, they can use their iPads with our new fabulous Wi-Fi services." She picked Percy up, as if he cared about Wi-Fi, or DStv or Netflix or whatever fandangle network service. He loved the cuddle and wrapped himself over her shoulder. This was his new home and he loved it – in fact, he was the happiest cat in the whole world.

The day 'the machine' arrived, was almost as big an event as the day the two lions arrived. It also arrived on a low bed truck early on a Thursday morning with flashing yellow lights one could see from far away through the early morning mist. Two engineers checked into Fiona's cottages the night before. They had to make sure that the machine was installed properly and that it worked according to plan. In preparation for the machine delivery, Troy received instructions to install two enormous steel rails upon which the entire contraption was going to rest. He assembled a team of workers from the local forestry and installed the rails exactly, to the millimetre, according to the requirements, along the length of the warehouse. In doing so, he left sufficient space for storage and packaging and even a little kitchen. Once he was satisfied that the rails were securely bolted into the new floor, he had the floor painted in a washable tennis court green, like he saw at the BMW factory when he was once taken on a visitor's tour.

One must give Troy credit. He took great pride in his work. When Fiona came to do a final check, she could not find a single thing that was overlooked. He had the old warehouse and even the staff toilets that stank of stale urine meticulously cleaned and repaired. His pride and joy, however, was the new gangway which was suspended from the roof by steel cables and anchored to the walls to make it sturdy. Two sets of steel steps on either side of the gangway gave it additional support. It was a simple, but effective design that was installed to provide an easy mechanism to service the machine's receiving hopper and conveyor belts. Strategically positioned lights, with football stadium reflectors, were fitted to illuminate the entire length of the machine, but less luminescence elsewhere in the warehouse. Troy was so excited about his project that he ran up the stairs to the middle of the gangway and shouted at Fiona: "Isn't this the most awesome space? We are going to make the most delicious kibbles in the country here. Look, I even had an extraction tube installed so that we can suck the hot air from the oven out of the building otherwise it will be unbearable in summer." He flung his arms around a huge silver painted pipe that extended all the way through the roof like a giant metal chimney and laughed with the delight of a toddler.

Fiona looked at Troy and grinned. She had a soft spot for him. Frankly, she had more than a soft spot for him and one could understand why. He was a good-looking man in his early forties, with dark, short cut hair and big muscular, tattooed arms that stretched his slightly undersized T-shirt sleeves to the maximum. Fiona often imagined that those big strong arms would keep her safe and protected from everything that could possibly go wrong in this world, especially after a few drinks at the Spit and Polish. When she was a little girl, her dad wrapped her in his arms and she felt safe there, protected and without a care in the world. When she stood on that washable tennis court green floor that day, looking at him holding on to the handrails from Bend-a-Tube, she felt a flutter in her chest and an overwhelming need to be protected again. She imagined how she would dig her face into his chest, hold his strong, swimmer's ribcage and cuddle the fuck out of him.

"It is fabulous. You have done a fabulous job," she said. She tried to control her trembling voice with a little cough which echoed through the empty space, then she wiped her mouth with a white tissue. "You can be proud of yourself Troy. When this thing is in full operation, we are going to make those lions very happy."

Troy laughed one of his exuberant laughs and said: "Don't mention it. We are in this together." The comment took her by surprise. What did he mean? Then he went on to say: "The only thing we still have to do is to finish the cobble paving in the parking area. I'm going to simply roll river stones into the ground with one of the municipality's road rollers. It will be firm enough for us and it will fit in with the environment."

"That's a great idea. I leave it in your capable hands, but would you mind if I go now? I am not feeling my best and would love a cup of tea."

Fiona, for once, looked unsure of herself.

"Sure, let's go. There is not much else to see here. I'll see you at Minnie's for tea and perhaps one of those decadent waffles."

On her way to the village, Fiona's left hand, as usual, found its way into the box of Urbanol in her hand stitched Matewis Maree shoulder bag on the passenger seat. She expertly freed a pill from the blister pack and swallowed the ten milligrams before she could taste the bitterness of the coating. Tea and waffles sounded like an excellent idea.

The installation of the machine was almost a non-event. After a little struggle through the forest on the dirt road, the low bed truck parked along the length of the warehouse. The driver and the two engineers expertly elevated the entire machine from the rear of the truck with a crane and heavy duty chains. I stood at a distance under the tree canopy and marvelled at the ease with which the crane operated. Next to the wheels were stabilising arms that dug into the ground to make sure that the entire truck did not fall over. Within a matter of minutes, they swung the machine through the side entrance and lowered it, centimetre by centimetre on to the rail which Troy installed. Within thirty minutes it was all over. The engineers then installed the feeder hopper and erected the conveyor belts on either side of the machine. All the equipment was secured with nifty clamps that reminded me of those twisted spring fasteners they used on railway lines. The electricity man from the municipality was put on standby to connect the machine to the main power supply, which he did in a few minutes. Just when I thought the whole installation was finished, the two engineers switched all the lights in the building off and started with a painstaking alignment process of the machine that lasted much longer than the whole installation. They used laser pointers and adjustment screws to make miniscule alterations along the entire installation from the receiving side, which was at ground level, to the last conveyor belt stand on the dispatch side, which was at hip height. From time to time Troy asked them questions to which they responded tersely. Troy just shook his head and allowed them do their thing, but he monitored their every move, presumably because he wanted to make sure that he would be able to repair the machine in an emergency. From what I could hear, the alignment was very important to ensure that the components inside machine matched up perfectly; so that the raw materials and kibbles would not get stuck or be deformed during the production process. The final part of the installation was the additives hopper, which was also somehow connected to the main processor at the start of the production process. It reminded me of the huge dough mixer I had seen at the bakery down the road from my house in the city.

It was very impressive, I thought.

At around lunch time, it was all done. Minnie arrived with a tray of food, which Fiona ordered. She walked curiously around the machine, which was standing there like a locomotive, ready to let off steam and blow its horn before embarking on a cross country journey.

"Goodness," she said, "what in heaven's name are you going to do with this monster Troy?"

"We will see this afternoon. It is going to be a big surprise, my friend," he said. "None of us, except those boys (pointing at the engineers) have ever seen how this thing works. I'm super excited."

While I stood there, I remembered how Fiona asked me to manage that outfit. Cold shivers ran down my spine. It was very exciting, but I did not know if I was cut out to do that kind of thing. When I saw how Troy ran up and down, holding spanners and asking questions, it occurred to me that he was much better qualified than me. I was too much of an artist. Sensitive and creative, I would say. Not made to run a factory or managing people, god forbid. I was the clean shaven hippie in nice clothes with my head in the stars that wanted to make the world a better place.

After the engineers completed the installation and devoured Minnie's homemade sourdough bread and a salad made of chicken breast chunks, Brie, strawberries and red cherry tomatoes, drenched with her secret dressing, they sat down with Troy, two of his workers and me to explain how the machine worked. There was the one hopper where the meat went in, another where all the other ingredients went in and a central processor that worked like a giant food processor that mixed and minced and mashed everything together into a paste that was squeezed through a shape and a cutter that formed the kibbles like cookies. The raw kibbles then went through an oven and came out on the other side as finished, healthy nibbles for the lions.

"What kind of meat can you put in this thing?"

I was surprised to hear Desfourneaux's voice behind me. He apparently listened to the entire orientation lesson. Since the crematorium incident, he lost even more weight and floated around like a shadow in his hugely oversized black suit.

"Any animal meat can be accommodated by the machine – beef, chicken, pork or lamb. The only reservation is that you must add as little hard bone as possible, such as the femur of a cow. The more bones you add to the processor, the higher your maintenance bill because they cause wear to the processor blades," the one engineer replied. The other one just looked at Desfourneaux and nodded. They both looked tired and irritable. "Are you ready to do a process run?" he asked.

"Yes," Troy said, "let's, do it brother! I found a recipe on the Internet for domestic cat kibbles. Hahaha! They say that cats have fairly strict nutritional requirements in terms of protein, calcium, phosphorus, and especially taurine, which is an amino acid, I think. I also read that a taurine-deficient diet can cause severe and possible fatal heart disease, so we better be damn careful with those furry babies on the farm. If you are ready, I'll call the

173

butcher. One of the cows on his farm was struck by lightning and he said we could have it. I checked with him and he said that he removed the skin and most of the bones and hooves because the people at the abattoir wanted it. Look brother, I also bought large quantities of the ingredients in the recipe which are in the store room."

Before anybody could say a word, he ran out of the room and came back with a trolley full of bags and other containers.

"It was a bit difficult to calculate what we would need because this recipe is in cups and spoonfuls, hahahahaha, so I thought we should get the weight of the cow and then calculate the rest of the ingredients with the spreadsheet that I made on my iPad."

"Yeah, that's exactly what we need," the engineer replied. "You can always refine the recipe at a later stage or even premix all the dry ingredients – which is better – then you can just add the meat."

I don't know how to describe my feelings about the so called dry run, because I was both horrified and amazed at the same time. The butcher arrived with the cow carcass, which was cut lengthwise in half. He and an assistant loaded it on a trolley which they wheeled to the edge of the feeder conveyor belt. In the meantime, I helped Matthew calculate and measure the ingredients (wheat flour, soy flour, wheat germ, cornmeal, non-fat dry milk, brewer's yeast, vegetable oil and cod liver oil) for our first batch of kibbles. I was much more comfortable with those ingredients than the gory stuff on the other side of the room.

Desfourneaux hung around like a janitor at a brothel. He slouched around in his dusty black shoes with his hands in his pockets peering over every shoulder, neither saying a word nor offering any assistance - occasionally licking his bottom lip.

At some or other time one of the engineers decided that it was time to start the machine. If it wasn't for the lights that shone in the oven and the low humming turning noise of the freshly greased mixer, one would never have known that it was alive. Once he was satisfied that the processor was running to his liking, he started the conveyor belts. They were a lot noisier but charming in a weird kind of way. I felt as if I was on a "How things are made" set.

The engineers checked the control panel out and pointed at the various options and configuration settings while explaining things in detail to Matthew and Troy. I could hear him going "yes, yes, I understand brother. Fucking hell, that is so awesome. I did not realise that it could do that! Sweeeeeeet!" He was like a little boy.

When the oven reached the correct temperature, a silver Land Rover parked outside. Shortly thereafter the boss woman came striding through the front door, cigarette in hand.

"Sorry lady," one of the engineers shouted, "this is a hygienic environment. Smoking is not allowed. Please smoke outside."

"Are you serious?" she said.

"Yes, madam, please go outside and by the way, language like that is not conducive to a healthy production environment."

Fiona was stunned. She turned on her heels and went outside. I bet she wished that she stayed outside because neither Fiona nor I were born to witness anything as hectic. The first of the carcasses was rolled on to the feeder belt. From there it slowly drifted upwards toward the feeder hopper. Matthew and I poured the rest of the ingredients into the other station and stood back. Nobody said a word. We all looked with the greatest of anticipation in the direction of that processor unit. When the carcass reached the gaping mouth of the feeder hopper all hell broke loose. At first there was a kind of slurping sound as the animal remains were sucked into the machine; then there were the sounds of bones being crushed and hammered. I guess it was the large lumps of crushed beef body that fell into the processor that made the machine shake and thump with a terrifying noise. By then the second half also arrived and the same routine was repeated. After, what felt like forever, the machine sucked the rest of the ingredients into the processor. It made the sound more muffled, like an old dog with a bone in front of a fire, growling and gurgling and slobbering. Finally, when the chopping came to an end, the machine went back to an easy rhythmic singing tone, similar to my mother's sewing machine.

My god, I thought. What kind of human being conceived of this grotesque machine that could decimate and destroy so quickly? Out of the corner of my eye I could see Fiona sitting on a box. She looked freshly fucked. Her hair was a mess, her lipstick was smudged and she shook like a leaf. Even though she looked as if she needed a blood transfusion, I deliberately did not look in her direction or talked to her, because I was equally traumatised. Troy, on the other hand, was hopping up and down with excitement, listening and looking and pointing at things, laughing in between. Desfourneaux just stood there, holding his hands in front of him as if he was hiding his manhood, just in case it might fall prey to the greedy machine's lust for meat.

"The paste is now at the right consistency," one of the engineers proclaimed. "You can look here." He opened a side panel. At the end of, what looked like a sausage spout, the kibble mixture was squeezed out and cut in perfect thickness. They came to a neat and perfect rest on another belt that ran slowly through the oven. The cooking process was completed quite fast, to my surprise. After about fifteen minutes the kibbles started to appear on the other side of the machine.

I picked one up. It was beautifully shaped like the claw of a lion, approximately ten times the size of commercial dog pellets. It was firm yet broke easily in my hand. Best of all, it smelt fantastic - in fact, it reminded me of a freshly cooked homemade hamburger patty.

"How fucking awesome is that! Fiona, come here! These food pellets are better than the ones you bought from the vet in the city. Just look here!" Troy took her hand and helped her to the machine. I could see she was not in good shape, but she did her best. Like a good sport, she followed him to the large heap of kibbles that poured out of her machine.

"Look," Troy said to her tenderly, "without you this would not have been possible. You are a rock star Fiona! Who would have thought about this but you?"

She smiled timidly and said: "C'mon guys! Time to celebrate! Let's quickly fill the bags and take them to the lions. Time for the consumer test!"

Later that afternoon, all of us except Troy sat at the best viewpoint overlooking the feeding spot at Panthera Park. All of us watched him fill the feeder silo, wondering if the lions would like the kibbles. Matthew came to sit next to me.

"Where have you been boy?" I asked.

"Sorry bro, I had to deal with issues at the distillery. I'll tell you about it later."

When Troy was finished, we could hear how he started the feeder and could see the food move towards the feeding bowls.

"Champagne everyone!" Fiona announced.

I took a bottle of bubbly out of the cooler box and corked it. By the time our glasses were full, the two lions woke up to the noise of the kibbles falling into the feeder. Troy ran as fast as he could across the cut grass to join us. He reached us just as the first lion decided to investigate her surroundings.

She walked lazily towards the feeding trough, sniffed and roared loudly. She then took a large mouthful of food and chowed them like chocolates. The other one soon followed.

"Thank you guys. You have done great work. From today we have a new product for the world. They are called Claws. Here's to Claws." Fiona held her glass up, we all clinked and drank to our achievement.

"Where is Desfourneaux?" Fiona asked. Nobody knew.

Over the next few weeks we carefully monitored the health of the Lions. The vets and the people from the Parks Board regularly came to inspect them and on one occasion even took blood samples. Troy eventually received a letter, signed by all of them, that the lions had made a complete recovery and that they highly recommended the facility for other organisations as a sanctuary.

Fiona cried in her handkerchief she was so happy.

Chapter 9

Fun and Games in the Forest

I think, following the installation of the machine, there was a collective sigh of relief in the village as well as a deep sense of accomplishment.

During the weeks that followed, we practiced and perfected the flow through the entire production line. Troy was a strict task master and made sure that things were done correctly. I felt uncomfortable on the production side and instead, became more and more involved with the admin side of the business, ordering supplies of all the ingredients, negotiating with the local farmers to acquire the corpses of their animals that died of natural causes. We maintained a strict rule that nothing would be killed for the machine.

Being somewhat artistic and practical, I also made sure that our Claws product was properly branded and stored in hermetically sealed containers to keep them fresh, and that only carefully calculated quantities went to Panthera Park to ensure that the food was always fresh and not wasted.

What none of us anticipated was the international sensation that our Claws product caused. Viewers from all over the world saw our fabulous kibbles, made from our secret recipe (that was, according to our marketing campaign, handed down over many generations), on the website's live feeds and the occasional live streaming on Facebook. Words of congratulations, encouragement as well as inquiries streamed in from all over the world – from the most pre-eminent zoos in the Unites States to the United Nations. Yes, the Unites Nations! They wanted to know if we could provide them with food that could be used in places where zoos were in distress following natural disasters and conflict. We even had an inquiry from a Middle Eastern billionaire who had a cheetah on his private yacht. He wanted to know if we could make kibbles from fillet steak, only, in the shape of his boat's insignia.

Of course, we said yes to all of them, which meant that the production time on the machine became longer and longer and longer and Fiona's pockets became deeper and deeper and deeper. Soon we introduced different flavours – donkey, horse and ostrich over and above the original beef flavour. Every time we introduced a new flavour, we made a big song and dance about it at Panthera Park, making absolutely sure that our followers on every single social network knew what we were doing.

One day, out of the blue, a white SUV, with a large antenna on the roof, appeared in the village, just as we made final preparations for the big party weekend. It stopped in front of the Spit and Polish. A man got out and asked where they could find Fiona. As it happened, she was at the chapel. A woman and a camera man got out of the vehicle and walked into the chapel where they interrupted a deep conversation between Fiona and Desfourneaux.

He had been suffering from severe depression following the crematorium explosion. As a result, he became more and more withdrawn and reclusive.

"I'm ruined, Fiona," he said. "The insurance people have all sorts of excuses why they don't want to pay for the fire at the crematorium. I also made a big mistake – I should have charged for cremations based on the new gas prices. The latest gas bottles cost twice as much as the previous ones. And since I no longer have a chicken farm, all my income has vanished. To crown it all, Mary Rose's family was very unhappy because I could not produce her remains soon after the funeral."

"I understand, but we can fix the crematorium," Fiona said.

"I cannot make a living burying old people. *Ils sont tellement avares!*" he shouted and banged on the bench with his bony fists.

Although she did not have a clue what he was saying, she understood more or less where he was going with the conversation.

"I'm not afraid of death Fiona. And if you work it right, you can make a good living out of it. I grew up with death. My father ran a bar in Algiers and made money on the side killing convicted Algerians. His godfather was

185

Algeria's high executioner. Beheading was in his blood. When I was fourteen, I made my father a miniature *guillotine*, which he had in his living room in *Fontaine-de-Vaucluse*, until he went insane, next to a cage in which he kept a parrot which sang the *Marseillaise*."

Fiona did not know if she was supposed to cry or laugh hysterically. Instead she bit on her lower lip and looked straight into the shadows where his eyes were supposed to be.

"I saw my first beheading at the age of 16, after my father asked me if I wanted to go to work with him. I stood to one side to keep out of his way. When we heard the call to prayer from the mosque round the corner, my father said, 'It's time!' Two guards brought the man out and pushed him on to the floor. I promise you Fiona, I saw his head go between the two uprights and a second later it was off! He did not even see the blade coming.

"After that execution, my father could see that I had the stomach for the business and I even worked for him for a while. It never worried me when we had botched executions, when the blade left a flap of flesh holding the head to the body. I even held the chopped off heads for the doctors who extracted the eyes with teaspoons for transplants immediately after the head was severed.

"My father taught me to keep a tight grip on the head during the execution. I used to hold them by the ears or hair because I was terrified that my fingers would be chopped off. When I was ready, I used to shout 'Go, father!' and - bang - the head was in my hands and I put it in the bucket. The blood used to shoot out like red wine. It was a good job. It gave me a feeling of power."

"Seriously Jannie? I feel nauseous. And you did that when you were a teenager?" Fiona gulped hard, "I cannot even page through the Grey's Anatomy I have in my bookstore. Didn't you feel sorry for the people you executed?"

"No, I never thought of the guy we guillotined. While you worked, you had to concentrate on your technique - and I always thought of the victims - what they went through. Through me they could achieve vengeance."

"My god! And you did that? I cannot believe it!" Fiona was horrified, not just by what he told her, but by the detached, callous manner in which he told her his story. He could just as well have told her how he counted coins as a bank teller.

"But ... were the people taken to the scaffold not scared?" she asked.

"Sure they were," he replied with the insouciant air of an art student, "some came out shouting and screaming, others were terrified, but when the blade fell, it was all over. Holding a head in my hands after an execution made a big impression on me that I can't really explain."

187

"And how did it happen that you ended up here?" Fiona asked.

"After my family were kicked out of Algeria, and the French gave up the death sentence, my father no longer had a job and I came here. At first, I got into a different form of execution - pest control," he said. "But I wanted a piece of land and when I found the farm at Cheerio, with a private crematorium on it, I knew it was a gift from the gods. But now it is in ruins and I can no longer serve my community."

Without warning Desfourneaux burst into tears that turned into sobs. He dug in his jacket inside pocket and pulled out a large white handkerchief, like a magician. Fiona stared at him and wondered when the multi-coloured ones would follow, but somehow felt sorry for him. He was, in a way the village clown – single, ostracised and sad. He never smiled, except at the bedside of a terminally ill person when he had all his paperwork signed. It must be difficult to function at the periphery of society, with a mind clouded by so many chopped off heads and especially those dead staring eyes, Fiona thought.

"I have a good therapist, who is an expert in regression hypnosis," she said. "Perhaps he can help you. No, on second thoughts, perhaps that is not such a great idea."

"I don't need a bloody therapist Fiona! I need money to fix the crematorium! Our dearly departed Mary Rose is still in the fridge and even though she is frozen, I'm sure she will start to go off soon. If the inspectors from the Department of Health had to do an inspection, I will be in unbelievable trouble and they will close down my business forever. That new machine of yours is parked on *my* property, in *my* warehouse and I suggest we start talking about a rental agreement."

After having unburdened himself of all his stresses, Desfourneaux started to shake wildly. Please, don't have a heart attack or die, Fiona thought. She could not deal with more complications and issues - with the major festival around the corner and the release of the new pork flavoured kibbles which she planned to coincide with all the publicity surrounding the trance party. She reached for the Urbanol in her Matewis Maree hand stitched shoulder bag and this time removed two pills from the blister pack.

"Swallow that! Now!" She gave Desfourneaux a pill but made sure that she had hers first and took a large gulp from her water bottle, before she gave it to him. There was no way on Earth she was going to drink from that bottle after him. He duly followed her instructions and after a while calmed down. When he regained his composure somewhat, he wiped his eyes clean with his hanky and put his solemn face back on.

"Look Jannie," she said, "we will make a plan immediately. Do you know who the suppliers of the kiln were? I'll get Troy and Max to help you make the arrangements. Don't worry about the insurance people. They are all a bunch of thieves – friendly when they come with their promises and paperwork, but tough as nails when you need help. I just do not know if we will be able to manage all of this before or during the festival next week, but I assure you on my mother's memory, that I will help you."

The two of them looked at each other in a moment of silence.

A female voice pierced through the quietness.

"Are you Fiona, sorry, I don't know your surname? Christina Amperboer. NNC News." She held her right hand out to greet Fiona and stuck a microphone in her face with the left hand.

"Hahahaha! Before you say anything, let me read you your Miranda rights. Anything you say, do or even think, will be either broadcast and or published in our Sleaze magazine, with or without your consent in whatever form I like!" She shrieked with laughter.

"What the …." was all that Fiona could utter. "Say again? What do you want from me?"

"Oh we want to know EVERYTHING!" Christina laughed one of those city girl plastic laughs that came out of her throat at half an octave higher than her speaking voice.

Fiona looked at her over her reading glasses. In front of her was a profoundly objectionable bitch of a woman in her mid-fifties who obviously had at least one botched facelift and about thirteen repair jobs which she tried to hide behind hair, straightened and coloured to the point that they could rival the hair at the Chinese Mall party shop. Her makeup was something to behold - every time she blinked, it looked like sunset over the Blyde River Canyon. She was slender and apparently shapely and firm – but one will never know if it was due to occasional exercise, liposuction or a substantial investment in cross your heart bras and cross your ass undergarments. Everything about that woman was artificial and ultimately disposable.

"Did you sleep with Elon Musk?" Christina said and shoved the microphone into Fiona's face.

"What are you talking about?"

"Yes, we know that he did special favours for you and we want to know why!" Christina was adamant to get a response out of Fiona.

"What was he like?" Christina giggled.

"Look you oestrogen charged, self-opinionated, self-important, overaged wannabe porn star - and you are welcome to broadcast that - you are invading my space and the sacred space in this chapel. You are not welcome here and I will not have you stick that metal dildo of yours in my face. Get out! Get out of here!" Fiona raised to her feet and towered over Christina in her high heels.

Taken aback, Christina was not prepared to give up that easily. "Now, now, no need to get tense! All I'm asking you to do is answer a few questions."

"In my day we used to execute harlots like her on the scaffold," Desfourneaux said. "They were always too loud for their own good. Perhaps her eardrums were damaged during the war."

Christina went white under her makeup.

"Did you hear me? I said get out of here!" Fiona shouted at the woman. By then the camera man was already waiting in the parking area.

"What's happening?" Troy saved the moment.

"Please get this woman out of here. She is harassing me." Fiona replied.

Christina left without a word, but vowed that she would find some smut about the village that she would publish for the world to see. If she could not find smut through Fiona, she would find it through the old man, she determined.

"Who the fuck is that?" Troy wanted to know.

"Some slag from some television station. I'll tell you later. Troy, please can I ask you and Max to *please* help

Jannie sort out that infernal crematorium? If that old woman is not cremated soon, there will be big shit."

"Sure, no sweat," he said.

The white SUV made a U-turn and headed back towards the Spit and Polish. They passed the square on the left. Opposite the chapel people were busy erecting a huge bandstand. Matthew called upon all his buddies in the industry to get a superb line-up of artists, which he personally met in the city to make the financial and practical arrangements. He also got hold of the people of Big Concerts to install the stage, lights, speakers and all the other things necessary to make everything work. It was going to be an intimate event as opposed to their normal standards and we wanted to take maximum advantage of the opportunity to get people to meet, greet and form friendships or even relationships. We also included a variety of other fun things, such as excursions to the waterfall, a barbeque at the rock pools, the zip lines, Panthera Park and walks through the forest as part of the weekend entertainment. Matthew even agreed to take visitors to the distillery.

As mysteriously as the SUV appeared, it disappeared again on the highway. Nobody knew that Christina and her camera man booked into the hotel in the middle of the forest.

That afternoon we got news from the only people we could find on the Internet who installed and maintained crematoriums in the area. They were able to help, but they required a lead time of two to three weeks to get the right people together for a job that far away from the city. They also needed to order consumables from abroad to service such an old kiln which would take time. Desfourneaux was in a state about it.

"Well my brother, we are just going to have to turn up that freezer of yours a couple of notches," Troy said to him. "They have found animals in the arctic that have been dead for thousands of years. As long as we keep her nice and cold, she will be all right."

Desfourneaux did not look convinced.

On my way home, I saw Matthew at Minnie's place.

"Wanna come with me to the distillery buddy?" he asked.

"Sure! I'd love to."

We took the road to Cheerio, drove past Desfourneaux's chicken farm, the little road that led to the crematorium and a couple of kilometres further, we turned into the rain forest along a well maintained gravel road. Matthew explained that it was a protected area and that nobody was allowed to disturb the vegetation. It was home to a wide variety of wild birds and animals. Many years ago, the locals marked clear hiking routes which visitors could follow to enjoy the best views through the valley and across the village.

Only the roof of the distillery was visible from the road. It was covered with solar panels. At the entrance was a huge replica of one of the Viper Premium bottles, expertly painted and decorated to look exactly like the real thing.

"How do you like my bottle bro?" Matthew asked.

"It is bloody incredible. I have never seen anything like that before."

"Cool hey? A mate of mine made it out of resin. We let all the incoming water from the river run through the bottle so that it always looks as if it is full of beer. There is also an air pump connected to it that makes bubbles. Hahahaha. You should see what it looks like at night. There is a light in the base that illuminates the whole thing. It is super cool, bro!"

We parked under an enormous tree.

"Welcome at my home and my work," he said. "Come let me show you around."

I followed Matthew along a paved walkway towards an old red face brick and concrete building that I could immediately see was immaculately renovated and maintained. The corrugated iron roof was painted in a dark red colour. In front of the building was a large square lawn with many canvass umbrellas, tables and benches.

"This place is hopefully going to be full of people next weekend." He laughed and looked around at me when we reached the entrance to the building. "Don't expect too much," he said. "We are still very small, but we are getting there. At the moment, we can produce around 650 litres of beer for every brew."

Behind the closed barn style door was a typical local pub, where people could socialise, taste the beer and buy more to take home with them.

"We hardly ever use the pub. People only really come here if they want to see how we make the beer. We are too far removed from the main road for people to use this as their local. That's why I also go to the Spit and Polish. "Come, let me show you ..." he said and opened a large, what appeared to be a steel door. I followed him into a cavernous room with four steel tanks and many interconnecting pipes and hoses.

"Beer starts with water bro. As you know, we have delicious clean mountain water, free of chlorine here. The water supply, which I showed you outside, comes in here where it is heated."

He pointed at the first tank.

"From there it goes into the mash tank, where we add malt, which is basically just germinated barley. We wait for the sugar in the barley to be released and when we are happy with the sugar content, we pump the brew into this unit which is the boiler." We walked to the next tank. "We add two types of hops – one to give it bitterness and the other to give it aroma. Once it has boiled for an hour, we cool the liquid down to about room temperature, add our special yeast, which I told you about and let it ferment for about a week. When there are enough bubbles, we bottle the beer at the end of the production line. That's all there is to it – but there are lots of tweaks and tricks in between. It took us a long time to make slight variations to the basic recipe." He looked at me proudly and grinned. "Anyway, that's what we show the public. I'm sure you want to see the off-limits stuff. Hahahaha."

"Wow, this is very impressive Matt," I said. "How many different types of beer do you make here?"

"Only two. One with and one without. Same recipe, one with added kick. Hahahaha. By the way – shall we have one?" Without waiting for an answer, he walked to the fridge behind the bar and opened two Viper Premiums for us.

I loved spending time with Matthew. There was a kind of relaxed gentleness about him that was drenched in wickedness.

"Are you scared of snakes?" he asked.

"I'm terrified of snakes."

"It's time to stop being scared of them. How are your tats, by the way?" He looked at me.

I was surprised that he asked. "They have become a little darker, but not much," I said.

"Before we go in, take your shirt off, let me have a look."

"Ok," I said and took my T-shirt off.

"Bro, I don't know what to say. You are going to be a legend. You have the most perfect patterns and markings I have seen. They are still pretty juvenile, but you can be super proud."

"What does it matter," I asked, "why are you looking at my markings?"

"Because they are fucking beautiful! You're lucky, you're close to shedding. Probably in a week's time. Exactly when we have the big party. With some extra work at the gym this week, I might get my shedding to happen with you. It will be something special." He ran the palms of his hands all over my back.

"How can you tell?"

"Your skin is starting to look and feel a little dull in a few places, like on your shoulders and hips."

I put my shirt back on. "It was really sore the last time. I better get to the doctor and get some pain medication before it happens again."

"No don't worry. It's only sore the first time. Very few people respond to the venom in the beer – almost all of them get drunk but nothing else – for some reason, every now and again, someone like you comes along and true magic happens. This is so cool bro, I'm so happy for you."

I smiled like a complete retard, because I had no idea what to expect and I did not have any idea what was happening to me, except that my skin was different and I noticed a change in the shape of the tip of my tongue that made me lisp every so often.

"Oh, and there is something else... but let me show you the breeding area first."

Matthew opened a door to a room the size of a large bedroom. A hot humid horrible musty odour, that smelt like a mouldy bathroom that had not seen the light of day for an eternity punched me in the face.

My first impression, apart from the smell, was the two walls of plastic containers that were stacked on top of one another to well above my height, in steel frames.

"We keep the juveniles in these containers. The ones on the left are the youngest ones and the ones on the other side are almost ready to be released outside." Matthew said. I cringed and felt cold, even though the room was hot and humid.

When I walked closer, I could get a view of the mulch-like substrate that was at the base of each box, together with saw dust, twigs and water. Matthew carried on to explain that there was at least one snake in each one of the trays. Every tray was mounted on a rail, which meant that it could be opened like a kitchen drawer, but thank goodness, it also had a firm lid.

"These snakes are eating machines," he carried on "but they don't have the swallowing ability that other snakes have because they are rather small adders. That is why we feed them on smaller prey – like a few pinks or fuzzy mice instead of one adult mouse. These babies only get pinks, even before their first shed."

I guessed he could see that I was less than impressed with his snake factory. "Isn't it horrible to feed them live creatures? I would hate having to do that," I said.

Matthew laughed.

"No these snakes are too small to eat live lizards or rats. After some trial and error we eventually settled on a diet of frozen rodents which we thaw in warm water before feeding time. The only gory thing that we have to do is to split the heads open so that the snakes can smell the food. Would you like to see? It's not dangerous, we give it to them with forceps."

"No, no, no! It sounds gross. It's suffocating in here." Sweat poured off my face.

"Oh, the temperature and humidity is controlled to provide them with perfect living conditions," Matthew said as he opened one of the trays. "Come have a look."

I could not believe that I got myself into this situation. The smells, the suffocating heat and just the thought of being surrounded by hundreds of snakes gave me the creeps. Frankly, the concept of breeding snakes and the mechanics of getting it done never, ever crossed my mind. Yes, I had seen snakes in captivity before, but I always just paid to get in, looked at them briefly and then left. I made a quick calculation to work out how many snakes were in the room with me. There were eight containers with ten levels on each side – that meant there were 1600 snakes in the room with us. 1600! What if there was an earth tremor and these containers fell over on top of us? What if someone deliberately sabotaged the trays? What would it feel like to try to get out in a hurry and there were hundreds of snakes on the floor? I needed one of Fiona's Urbanols.

"Come on, there is nothing to be scared of brother. I'll make sure you are safe at all times. We have to be safe here. We even have safety drills, just like fire drills in an office block. Anyway, these babies are too small to get their teeth into you. Their venom is also not strong enough to kill an adult. I told you that I was out of it for a week and I have a slight facial paralysis as a result of my run-in with the snake in the Drakensberg, and that one was fully grown."

201

I looked into the tray. In front of us was a baby Berg Adder, chilling all by itself. It was alert and moved when Matthew touched it with a stick, but did not appear to be phased by our presence. As I looked at his hand, holding the stick and the patterns on the snake, it occurred to me that the markings on his fingers were almost identical to the ones on the baby. The back of my own hand and the faint geometrics on my fingers looked strikingly similar – similar enough to let me feel some kind of bizarre affinity with the creature in the box – as if we were related in some way.

"If you read up on the Internet, you will see that these snakes are referred to as irascible and that they hiss violently and twist convulsively if one disturbs them. Look, this little one is calm and not stressed at all with us around. Amazing hey?"

"Why is that? Is he sedated?"

"No stupid," he laughed me. "Come let's get out of here. I want to show you the adults."

Matthew closed the lid and pushed the tray back into the wall of containers. Another brick in the wall, I thought. Having had a look at the snake somehow made the fear and the cringe go away; instead I felt respect, a respect that kept me at a distance, a safe distance. That was all that was needed. We needed to respect each other's space. A kilometre radius space sounded good to me.

"One day, when we have time, and you are less squeamish, I'll show you the place where we prepare their food and how we milk them," Matthew said and grinned at me.

We walked back through the bar and around the outside of the building. A little removed from the main building was a large square structure with a half-height wall and a thatched roof that covered it like a giant square umbrella. A paved walkway, made of interlocking bricks surrounded the building. Matthew was visibly excited, but I was merely relieved that I was out of that stuffy room and could breathe more easily. So now I know, I thought, what snake shit smelt like – that must have been the odour that permeated that whole room. How revolting! Mind you, if you caged a large amount of humans into a small space, I guess it would smell just as bad.

"Come check this out brother," Matthew called me over to where he stood next to the wall. "This was the first enclosure we built for the few snakes which we brought from the Drakensberg. All of them were adults."

"How big does and adult get?" I wanted to know.

"Not much more than half a meter."

Inside the enclosure was indigenous wild grass and rock that resembled the countryside. When I first looked, I did not see anything, but then I noticed a snake stretched out along the wall, right next to me.

"There are sixty-six adults in here." Matthew said with a big smile. "All male. You should have fun in there! Hahahaha!"

"Fuck you, that's not funny. I cannot imagine anything worse than going in there. Eeeeewww!"

"Now let me tell you. Those snakes will not do anything to you, not even if you annoy them," he said. "Snakes do not bite one another. That is why you will see these snakes ignore each other. If you are not food, threatening or a predator, it is of no interest to a snake – unless it is the mating season."

"That's interesting. Don't they fight or bite each other in mating season?" I asked.

"No not at all. During mating season, the males will wrestle with one another, but they will not bite each other. Venomous snakes are in any case immune to their own venom. Think about how often you may have bitten your lip, tongue, or inside of your cheek, and your teeth are not even mobile like most venomous snakes are. There's a significant chance of a snake accidentally biting itself, and that's why snakes have developed an immunity to their own toxin. This apparently extends to closely related species. If one species used the same enzymes in their venom as a completely different species used in their venom, chances are they would be immune to each other's venom."

"I never knew that. I thought that they could kill each other with their venom," I said.

"Not true buddy," Matthew replied. "But I have to qualify what I am saying. Not all snake venoms are the same, some are neurotoxic, hemotoxic, necrotising, or anticoagulant. Even within these general groups, not all species use the same enzymes in their toxins. If the enzymes in their venom are different, then it is a completely different story. Certain snakes will use that to their advantage when they prey on other snakes."

"But, if I understand you correctly, the snakes in this pit will not bite each other and even if they do, they will survive?"

"Yes, you've got it bro. But the interesting thing is that you and I can go in there and they will consider us to be one of their own and not do anything to us. If anybody else, who has not gone through the changes we have gone through go in there, the snakes will see them as threatening and strike at them."

I could not believe what he was telling me. "You're shitting me!"

"I'll prove it to you," he said and took his shoes off. Before I could say anything or object, he opened a door along the side of the enclosure and walked into the snake pit with sixty-six snakes inside.

"Matthew, no! Please don't. Please! I can't stand this. What if what you are saying is not true? I have no idea how to help you if you get bitten. Please come out of there," I begged.

"Don't stress my friend. Look here." He picked up a big fat snake that was, I guessed fully grown, and held it up as if he was testing a string of spaghetti to see if it was *al dente*. My heart raced and I'm sure my blood pressure went through the grass roof. At that moment I noticed another one uncoil next to his foot and moved its head over Matthew's foot. I was beside myself.

"Matthew, look out, by your foot! Do you enjoy freaking me out like this?!"

"Ok, I guess I have proved my point. I'll come out." He gently put the snake down and let it move away into the grass. The other one took no notice of him and also made its way into the grass. When the two snakes crossed paths, they acknowledged one another's presence and gently moved along in search of food or whatever snakes search for – perhaps the meaning of their slithering lives. What the hell?! Did I become like them? Am I now a snake big brother?

On our way out, we walked past the bar, where he grabbed two more cold Viper Premiums for us. I felt shaky and confused and dare I say, traumatised by the event. Matthew could see that I was not at my best and put his arm around my shoulder.

"Ok let me show you where I live," he said. "It's just up the road from here. We could walk there, but let's rather drive, because we have to go back into the village later."

We followed the dirt road against a steep incline to his house.

What we did not notice, was the white SUV with the antenna, parked behind a large bush. Unbeknownst to us, the occupants followed our every move and captured our movements at the snake pit with paparazzi lenses.

"I'm convinced they are storing drugs in that building," Christina said to the cameraman, who doubled up as her driver. "They look like a bunch of hippie weed heads!"

Christina was an old hand at sniffing out shit about people and she was convinced that there were shenanigans going on which she wanted to expose just like she exposed her saggy ass in *Lycra* pants.

"Let's have a look. There is nobody here."

She did not wait for a response from the cameraman, nor did she hesitate when she walked down the interlocked brick pathway or when she walked past the snake warnings on the wall or opened the gate to the adult snake enclosure. She stepped into the stockade and by sheer luck ended in the middle of the space unscathed.

"What is this place?" She said, "There is nothing in here. Just grass. These people should learn to keep their properties clean. I cannot believe …. Ugh! C'mon, switch your cine lights on. Shine them here by my feet – I cannot see a damn thing."

What can I say? This was Christina's worst phobia come true. All her life she had been terrified to the point of collapse of snakes. Once, when she was a little girl, she watched a program on television about a King Cobra, sitting cross legged on her little baby chair right in front of the screen. At one stage the cobra lunged at the camera. Little Christina got such a fright that she jerked, fell over backwards and hit her head badly against the coffee table. Her mother rushed into the room to help her. By the time she stood up and her tears dried away, she saw the king snake biting deep into and then swallowing a rat snake.

That night she dreamt that her mother arranged a huge birthday party for her. She looked pretty in her little pink dress, two strings of platted hair and pink ribbon bows. The tables were full of delicious snacks and lemonade, her mother made during the early hours of the morning, while she was still sleeping. She found herself surrounded by an enormous amount of gifts, beautifully wrapped in gorgeous paper with beautiful ribbons tied in perfect bows. When her mother said it was time to open her presents, she picked a box, put it between her legs and pulled the ends of the ribbon to untie the knot. The ribbon turned into a thin snake in her hands. She tossed the snake across the room, screamed and jumped up. She tried to open a second box but it was also decorated with a ribbon snake. Again she screamed and let the snake get away. Like a good little girl, she tried another box, and another, because she so badly wanted to see her gifts, but every box had a ribbon snake wrapped around it. There were bright green ones, blue ones, pink ones, light brown ones and ones with beautiful patterns, but they had nasty open mouths with huge teeth and long forked tongues that terrified her. In the end she ran upstairs to her bedroom where she could hide from the hundreds of snakes in the sitting room. When she looked in the mirror next to her bed, she tried to take the ribbons out of her hair – but they too turned into nasty spitting snakes that curled around her fingers and her neck. Her mother mercifully woke her with a cup of tea – it was time to go to school. From that day onwards Christina feared snakes more than the devil itself. She refused to see movies or documentaries about snakes, let alone snake parks and sanctuaries. Before going into the countryside, she made double and triple sure that there were no snakes about and now she found herself in a snake pit with hissing and spitting reptiles that found her equally terrifying.

Christina's vitriolic thoughts instantly moved out of her mind in deference to her survival when she realised that she was surrounded by real venomous snakes with v-shaped heads and evil eyes. They in turn gave her as much attitude, hooding and hissing, exactly as described in the article Matthew found on the Internet. She turned into a screaming concrete pillar, standing there motionless while the cameraman filmed the spectacle. She shrieked at the top of her voice, which echoed through the valley. Her screams were so tortured and desperate that Matthew and I heard her over the growling of the engine, as we negotiated our way up the hill. Matthew immediately stopped and turned around.

"I don't know who that is, but it sounds serious bro," was all he said. We both looked straight ahead in an attempt to work out where the screams came from. We eventually parked almost where we were less than ten minutes earlier and ran towards the open snake enclosure where the shrieks of terror came from.

"Whatever you do, don't move lady or you will be bitten! Don't look down. Stop screaming, stop screaming! We are here to help you." By then several other people also arrived.

Christina calmed down somewhat but kept hyperventilating.

Matthew calmly and extremely slowly walked into the enclosure.

"I'm coming to you, but I have to move these boys out of the way one at a time. They are very agitated and I don't want both of us to get nailed, so pretend you are standing in the queue at the bank. You are safe for as long as you don't move..."

With bare hands, Matthew picked up a snake at a time and moved them out of the way to create a walkway for him and Christina. Fortunately, snakes, like most other creatures, instinctively move away from danger. By the time he reached her, which felt like an hour later, she was drenched in a cold sweat and shaking uncontrollably.

"I'm not strong enough to pick you up and even if I tried and I dropped you - because you are wet and slippery - you are going to be in bigger shit. So you can either walk out with me now or I can get someone to fetch you a pair of wellies, but that is going to take a little while. Can you hold on to me and walk out with me?"

A little squeak came out of her mouth which Matthew interpreted as yes.

"Ok, put both your hands on my shoulders. I will make sure the path is clear. C'mon, you can do it."

Matthew gave one step forward and she gingerly followed in her high heel open shoe. He looked around, and gave another step forward. She followed, step at a time, until they finally set foot on safe territory. The moment that she realised that she was out of the snake pit, Christina collapsed. A few people helped, picked her up and rushed her to Dr Riaan. He gave her a tranquiliser and sent her home to get some rest.

That night, just when the half-moon rose over the valley, screams were heard coming from Christina's room at the hotel. Her nightmares had come back to haunt her.

Chapter 10

Crunch Time

The big weekend finally arrived.

Minnie, who managed and monitored all the ticket sales through the Internet, reported a week before the event that all the tickets and accommodation were sold out. Even the horrible caravan park, a few kilometres away, was filled to capacity. During that week, everyone involved with the preparations was visibly stressed, except Troy and Matthew. They loved helping with the assembly of the craft beer stalls and spent as much time as possible tasting and talking to the exhibitors.

Viper Beer dominated the beer section with a huge illuminated beer bottle, similar to the one at the distillery entrance, but this time beer was tapped from it for everyone who danced or worked up a thirst. Large trucks arrived with provisions, from toilet paper to toothpics. Minnie's stock room was filled to the brim with ingredients for her delicious range of new dishes, which she had printed on a twofold menu. I helped her page through a variety of Facebook recipe pages with quick and easy meals. From there we selected a few that were the most popular, tried them out and included them for the big event. On the Wednesday before the event, I went to her restaurant where she gave her staff a briefing session. I wished that managers at my work in the city understood how important it was to really care for employees the way she did. She did a final test run with the chefs to make sure their timing was right and that the food was memorable enough to bring people back when the party was over. The front of the restaurant was equally busy. Minnie invited the locals to taste the food and suggest improvements. Needless to say, everybody thoroughly enjoyed the evening and were blown away by the tasty new treats Minnie added to her repertoire.

At the end of the evening Minnie appeared in the kitchen door with a glass of white wine. She looked exhausted, with a huge grin on her face. Every single person in the room got up and clapped hands, shouting words of congratulations and adoration. That evening I noticed a kind of impishness about her that I had never noticed before. When I looked at her, standing there in her farmwife dress, mercifully covered by a white apron, holding an almost empty glass of wine in her hand, I became convinced that she was a closet party girl that never got the chance to let go.

Minnie somehow became the mother of the village – she was the face of charm, kindness and an uncanny drive to succeed with her little business - which she did indeed. The ovation caught her off-guard and momentarily reduced her to tears, which she dried with a large white napkin that was tucked to her waist.

"Thank you. I was so scared and this is such an important occasion for all of us. I did not want to just have waffles and hotdogs on the menu, but I also did not want to come across as pretentious and grand, so if you approved of your meals, then I think we found the right mix, if you will pardon the pun." She started to giggle at her stupid little joke and laughed - almost hysterically. All we could do was laugh with her until we doubled up.

"I'm so happy!" she shouted, with a fist in the air, in between the fits of laughter, "this weekend we are going to party the hell out of this place! I cannot wait! Thank you everyone. Thank you so very, very much."

I guessed the tension that built up in the village was released to a degree that evening.

The guests started to arrive shortly after lunch on Friday. It was a balmy, windless autumn day with just enough cloud in the sky to cast large polka dots of shadow over the village and surrounding areas. Troy had a 'welcome gate' installed at the entrance where all visitors were checked in and directed to their accommodation. He recruited four muscle boys from the forestry school to man the entrance. Just to get the visitors in the right frame of mind, the boys were dressed only in khaki shorts and rock climbing harnesses. Once the visitors were signed in, the boys strapped a party band around their arms and sealed the deal with a tequila.

217

The cottage, inn and guest house owners took over from there. Before the visitors arrived, the gate boys let them know using a brand new app that was designed and built especially for the event. It required some gruelling training for a few technically challenged locals (who could hardly fathom the concept of an email) to become fully proficient with the new way of handling a client by phone. Fiona emphasized that all the staff should memorise their guests' names before they arrived.

"You have to be customer focused," she said to her own staff and the house keeper. "These people must feel as if you prepared everything for them and them only. They must feel as if they have just booked into a five-star hotel in Thailand."

None of her staff members ever booked into a five-star hotel and I am pretty sure none of them knew where Thailand was on the map, but they understood that the visitors had to be pampered like grandchildren on Christmas Eve.

Upon their arrival, visitors were welcomed to rooms, freshly cleaned and manicured using Fiona's expert guidance and financial assistance. The Ginger Cat girls delivered the most gorgeous, sumptuous linen and blankets. When I saw my cottage after it was upgraded, I just wanted to roll around on my bed and enjoy my new creature comforts. Fiona cleverly made sure that the rooms looked comfortable and inviting, rather than smart and repellent. Earlier in the day, she told the cleaning staff to bake an apple with cinnamon and vanilla essence in the room ovens that shrouded all the rooms in delicious homely smells that made me feel relaxed and hungry.

Before I went out that evening I had a nap with Percy rolled up next to me. I knew that it was going to be a big weekend, so I made sure that I was rested enough to have as much fun as possible.

Nothing could have prepared me for the visual spectacle that unfolded that evening. Troy, Matthew and all their helpers created a veritable fairyland that took me and everyone who came to visit by surprise – from the colourful lights that lined the entrance into the village, which were cleverly positioned at knee height – to the hundreds of colourful hammocks all along the edge of the rain forest, where party goers could chill and literally hang out and chat and relax. The forest floor under the hammocks was beautifully cleared and illuminated with minute lights that created a magical fairyland. Many people spread blankets amongst the trees and made new friends.

The umbrellas that normally provided shelter during the day were folded and moved out of the way to allow a variety of laser lights to play with the stars; dancing around the chapel tower that changed colours in harmony with the music.

219

Ashlinn Gray opened the line-up at exactly six in the evening, just as the sun was setting, with her famous song 'Battleships'. People came from everywhere to look at this beautiful woman with the awesome voice. She flicked her long blond hair with the arrogance of a youngster as she sang her signature tune. She certainly did not have to work hard to get the crowd fired up – they knew the words and went wild as soon as the acoustic guitar announced the song.

"I won't surrender ah ah ah, ah ah ah ah
Not sending out an S.O.S
I won't surrender ah ah ah, ah ah ah ah
Not sending out an S.O.S

Every word you throw at me, can't hurt me anymore
Was down but I got up, won't lose cause I'm fighting for,
a chance to live each day
I'm giving it my all, moving on without the fear I felt
before ..."

I was in my element and loved being there. According to Minnie's statistics, around 70% of the crowd were single. Great, I thought, that there were so many. Even though I knew it was not true, I always thought of myself as the only one that was alone and had to make peace with the fact that relationships were as disposable as empty water bottles. They also caused as much pollution, I thought and laughed by myself.

We had very specific responsibilities for the evening. Troy was responsible for safety and all crowd movement; from the security gates to the residential areas and the village square, where everything happened. Matthew was responsible for entertainment, the lights, the acts and all the technical stuff that was required to make the event possible. Dr Riaan was put on standby for medical emergencies, for which two rooms in the frail care section of the old age home were reserved. Fiona was in charge of accommodation and client services. Troy had a large tent erected between Minnie's restaurant and the Spit and Polish, complete with a Persian carpet and two large couches and a coffee table where Fiona could talk to the press, television and visitors to the village. We all relied on her to expertly advise them on financial matters, especially the benefits of the Indulge Card, as well as investment opportunities in the lion adoption scheme, over and above the lifestyle and entertainment that was available in the vicinity. She was a professional through and through. Paul and Minnie were in charge of food and drink. It was astonishing to see the speed with which they served everyone. The Indulge Card phone app that managed the village activities also allowed people to execute transactions with a finger print only. No money or cards were exchanged. Guests could take what they wanted, approve the transaction with a touch on their phone's home button and have more fun.

"Standing in long queues at events like these is the kiss of death," Fiona said to the software developer, while waving her cigarette around. "You better write me a fabulous little application that will take the queues away. I want people to dance, not queue." And so he did. There were no gatherings at the booze counters. We maximised our opportunities – we hit the iron with a sledgehammer while it was hot – so to speak.

Since Matthew took care of the entertainment and entertainers, he asked me to take care of the Viper Beer stand.

"Don't worry about how the beer is made or what we put into it," he said. "At this stage of the game people just want to get pissed and have a good time, so try and sell as much as possible, but don't sell the Premiums - they are for us for later." I did not know what to make of his last comment, but I nevertheless saved the Premiums under the table. There was not much to do. People came to ask for six-packs, I scanned the wrapper and they closed the deal with a fingerprint. It was simple and supremely efficient. It also gave me ample time to look around and enjoy the vibe.

At around eight, I noticed the woman who was saved from the snake pit. She and the cameraman walked around the outside of the dancefloor, occasionally pointing and talking. They eventually went into Fiona's tent. From what I heard later, there was a very unpleasant confrontation. Fiona did not take kindly to the fact that Christina just walked into her tent while she was engrossed in a private conversation with a possible investor. By then she was reasonably well lubricated, after an excellent bottle of Chardonnay. No wonder that she had little patience with the plastic doll that wanted to be famous. Word has it that she had Christina forcibly removed from her tent by two body builder lumberjacks. Apparently everything happened so quickly that the cameraman did not even get any footage of the altercation. When the two of them emerged from the tent, Christina caused a major scene and swore revenge. They were last seen walking towards the main entrance.

Nobody paid attention to her and her little drama. The guests loved the acts that followed and became more and more animated in anticipation of the main event of the evening.

The only person who felt completely out of place was Jean-Henri Desfourneaux, the mayor. He did his best to contribute to the success of the festival by using his organisational and management skills at the municipality. He also facilitated all the planning meetings, but the event itself did not mean much to him. He was worried, you see. He had a corpse in the fridge that needed to be disposed of urgently. Exasperated by the noise and the people and the drinking and the shouting, he got into his SUV and headed out of the village.

The security people recognised his vehicle and briefly greeted him on his way out. "Good evening sir, are you sober enough to drive? We have breathalysers here for your convenience, just in case."

The courteousness got on his nerves. "Get out of my way! I did not drink. I had to work."

"Very well sir, drive safely."

Little did they know that Desfourneaux had secretly given up all hope that he would find answers to the issues that plagued him and for which he simply could not work out satisfactory answers. Too many things went wrong. Too many things he simply could not control. Yes, the festival appeared to be a big success and the lion kibble business seemed to generate lots of cash, but there was also a mountain of debt to service following the improvements that were made everywhere. That bitch of a Fiona wanted her cash back first, for the dreaded machine, the warehouse alterations that Troy so happily went and did without his approval and even the packaging and marketing sprees which cost a ridiculous amount of money. He was old school. His father taught him to chop one head off at a time and not make a big spectacle out of it. Hold it down and keep your fingers out of the way. Business had to start small and grow big. This new generation that could create a living out of phone apps was beyond him – it was improbable and out of this world to say the least. In the end he concluded that he had to start somewhere small to get his life back in order. One step at a time. It no longer mattered to him what others thought, his own survival became more important than anything else. And he was going to make it happen on his own while everybody was having a party. At the highway intersection he turned right towards the forest and then followed the road to Cheerio. It was his chicken ranch that went wrong, but subsequently became the home of Fiona's infernal machine. He felt ambivalent about that machine. On the one hand, it held the keys to their success, but it also emasculated him, robbed him of his privacy and made him subservient to Fiona on his own property.

He opened the large sliding doors and stared at the machine for a moment. He no longer feared the thing, he had seen how Troy and Matthew operated it. He switched the low lights on next to the entrance and then flicked the main start-up button to get the machine going. Fortunately, the monster was pre-programmed to manufacture and roast the kibbles to perfection, so there was not much to do except mix the ingredients. When he was satisfied that the machine was warmed up, he turned around and walked out of the building – determined and purposeful.

While Desfourneaux was going about his business, the white television vehicle pulled up outside and parked behind some thick vegetation.

"There is something underhanded going on," Christina whispered to her cameraman earlier when she saw Desfourneaux leave the village. "I'm going to follow him. You stay here and see what you can come up with. Give me the GoPro."

When she saw Desfourneaux walk out of the building she decided to sneak in and check him out from the gangway above the machine. I should have a good view from there, she thought; it is also dark up there - that old man will never see me.

She shut the car door quietly and ran from one dark spot to the next, like she saw the SWAT people do on television. When she got to the front door, she quickly scanned the inside to see if there was anybody waiting for Desfourneaux to come back. There was nobody. She slipped off her high heels and ran across the floor and up the steel steps to right above the machine. While she felt safe, she took a few pictures with her phone and then put the GoPro camera on a selfie stick, so that she could get a perfect view from above.

She had to wait for quite a while before Desfourneaux came back, but when he eventually arrived, Christina was shocked. Desfourneaux looked like death. At the doorway he had a coughing fit, pulled out his asthma pump and sucked greedily on the spout. He pulled a trolley behind him. Christina reached over the railing to see what was on the trolley, but it was covered in a grey blanket and she could not make out what it was. If a frail old man like Desfourneaux had to get that thing on the trolley, then he possessed supernatural powers, she thought. And she was right. The effort required a monumental effort on his part.

While Christina waited for him, Desfourneaux manoeuvred the trolley into the fridge and parked long ways next to the coffin of dear Mary Rose. She was on the middle shelf, about a meter above the trolley. If only he could get her out of the coffin and on to the trolley, he would be ok, but he was frail and she was large. After he evaluated all his options, he concluded that his only option was to turn the coffin on its side and let her frozen body roll on to the trolley. It was a bit rough, but he could not think of another plan. He looked around for some kind of cushioning to dampen her fall, but there was nothing, so he went for it. After searching around, he found a metal bar that strong enough to unseat the coffin. He hooked it under the casket like a tyre leaver and pulled with all his might.

When it eventually turned, the lid gave way and Mary Rose fell from that shelf like an iceberg. Her head took the full force of the impact and snapped off just above the shoulders. The rest of her body hit that trolley with the impact of a sledgehammer.

"Oh dieu, ma douce mère, Maria," he mumbled, staggered around the shelving and picked up Mary Rose's

head. Her eyes were shut but it felt if she stared at him. As he stood there, holding her by her frozen hair, dotted with icicles, he could not help but stare right back at her, like he stared at the heads at the guillotine. They looked at each other for a while, from two completely different worlds. Shaken by the trauma he inflicted upon his client, Desfourneaux whispered "I'm so sorry my dearest Mary. I did not mean for you to lose your head like all those bastards on the scaffold. I'm so sorry."

He straightened Mary Rose's body on the trolley and placed her head on her chest with her long stringy grey hair spread neatly arranged over her torso. He then retrieved the carcass of his dog and placed it between her legs, before he covered them in a blanket.

By the time he arrived back in the machine room with his cargo, it was warmed up, he was exhausted and Christina was frantic. He wheeled the trolley to the loading conveyor belt and sat down to catch his breath. Christina craned her neck and held the selfie stick with the little GoPro camera, which she strapped around her arm, as far out as possible to get the best view of Desfourneaux. After a few minutes, he regained his strength and with singular determination started with the final part of the process.

The first and easiest to go onto the conveyor belt was the dog, then the head of Mary Rose. From a distance they looked remarkably similar to Christina, who at that stage

228

could not quite work out what she was witnessing. Thanks to Troy, the trolley and the conveyor belt were at the same level, which meant that he only needed to slide Mary's headless body on the conveyor belt. Again, Desfourneaux used his stick to lever the old woman's body into position. With the last energy left in his body, he managed to manipulate her from the flat surface to the moving belt.

"Goodbye my friends. You are going to a good home," he said.

As the dog body, the head and finally the body of Mary Rose moved up the conveyor belt to the feeder hopper, Desfourneaux put on his funeral director face and in his mind prepared to recite the Lord's Prayer.

From where she stood, Christina could see when the dog approached the hopper. When it went into the machine, there were a few loud thuds and crunch noises. With some careful manoeuvring Christina captured the event on video.

When Mary Rose's head arrived, Christina realised that this was not another dead dog. The naked body that followed was certainly not part of an animal – she could tell from the large tits that were firmly frozen, pointing at the heavens. She went out of her mind. It was a much bigger story she had ever imagined. It was going to make her famous, more than any atrocity she had ever covered in the Middle East or her intimate interview with Tony

229

Blair at the Wailing Wall. For the second time in two days, her blood pressure reached pathological levels as the 'goods' entered the mouth of the feeder hopper.

Desfourneaux turned his back upon the machine, closed his eyes and folded his bony hands.

"Our Father in heaven,
hallowed be your name.
Your Kingdom come,
your will be done,
on earth as in heaven ..."

It was an ideal opportunity for Christina to milk the situation as far as possible. She clearly saw how the black dog was sucked into the machine, but she was not prepared for the thuds and bangs that stemmed from the crusher when Mary Rose's head went through the hopper. It dropped like a rock and bounced back for just long enough to get that stringy grey hair to wrap around the GoPro with the might of steel. It then went back into the machine, banging and crushing, pulling on the camera, the stick and Christina. She lost her balance.

"Give us today our daily bread.
Forgive us our sins,
as we forgive those who sin against us.
Lead us not into temptation,
but deliver us from evil."

It happened instantly; Christina did not see it coming. The one moment she was holding the camera so that she could film Rose's head disappear into the bowels of the machine, the next moment, she was yanked off the railing and fell head first into the feeder. She did not see the blade. She did not feel anything. She did not even make a noise as she departed into eternity, minced and freshly grounded.

"For the kingdom,
the power and the glory are yours.
Now and for ever.
Amen."

That is how Christina and the dog were joined by Mary Rose whose frozen journey mercifully came to an end that evening. The machine crunched and blended them and the other ingredients into a perfect paste that produced the most delectable Claws a few minutes later. Desfourneaux had no clue what had happened. He was not even aware that there was someone in the building.

When it was all over, the old man made an effort to clear his tracks; he poured the Claws into fresh bags, sealed them and saved them in the warehouse. At sunrise, the morning staff collected the kibbles and fed them to the lions at Panthera Park. When Troy tasted one of them a few days later, he said that they were sweet and sour. I never tried them out.

The only evidence that was ever found about Christina's presence in that building was a pair of green high heel sandals on the gangway.

Later that evening Desfourneaux scraped some ash out of Darth Vader at the Spit and Polish into a shoebox. While the crowd went wild for Prime Circle, he went home and crunched the ash into a fine powder, then decanted it into an urn with a metal plaque inscribed with the words Mary Rose. He could finally put the nightmare behind him. Despite the raucous music and celebration in the village square, Desfourneaux slept really, really well that night. He was content and relaxed after he completed his unfinished business.

The cameraman, delighted to be free for a while, followed his nose and eventually found his tribe. They sat in a circle in the woods and talked shit. Between them were remnants of fresh hydroponic weed and roaches. A very slender girl with long dark reddish hair invited him to sit down and share a couple of beers and a bong. "Hi, I'm Candy, we are all a bunch of band fans," she said in a high pitched voice. He noticed how limp her eyelids were when she passed the appliance to him. Their fingers touched briefly as he took it from her. When their eyes locked as well, she giggled and wiggled her toes.

"[giggle] Oeeeee! This is heaven!" she said. He too was in heaven soon after that.

In the meantime, I dutifully and completely unaware of what went on, manned the Viper beer stand. As the night wore on, a few dumb asses came to talk to me. I guess it was supposed to be a hook-up weekend, but I was not on the menu – unless someone exceptional turned up. But that did not happen. The crowd went wild when Prime Circle concluded with their song Ghosts. The moment they finished their gig, half of the people on the dancefloor ran into the woods to have a pee and the other half came to look for drinks.

While I served beer to a queue of people, I heard Troy's voice on the speakers.

"Howzit everyone! What's happening hey?" The crowd responded with shouts of approval and whistling. I wished that I could whistle like the local farmer boys could.

Troy laughed one of those broad laughs that made him look taken by surprise and shy at the same time.

"Fuck you too!" He shouted back at the crowd. "How dare you whistle at me? I'm no cheap trick!"

They laughed at him. "Now listen, you ball bags, there is no time to take it easy. We are going to rock you until you are cooking on high in a few minutes. So, empty your bladders and fill up your drinks, the party is about to start. But first, I would like to make a couple of announcements. Thank you to everyone who made this

233

possible – I'm not going to mention your names, but I'd like to call Fiona and Matthew to come up here."

From where I stood, I could see Fiona and Matthew getting on stage. Fiona looked sensational. She was dressed in black from head to toe – I could not believe it - she looked like a panther in a skin-tight top and black super skinny jeans and high heel black boots. I always suspected that there was something brewing between her and Troy, and at that moment understood why he saw Fiona more like a MILF than a business woman. I grinned by myself and was happy for the two of them.

"This lady," Troy carried on, "made a massive investment in this event, the village and at Panthera Park next door, which is a sanctuary for lions and, perhaps one day, other wild cats too." He winked at Fiona, who still had no idea what this was leading up to.

"Well, I have a major announcement to make, the British Charity, Lion Defenders International, let us know tonight that Panthera Park was selected as their preferred sanctuary, following the successes she achieved with the lion food, which we produce down the road from here, as well as the charity debit card called Indulge, which I hope you all acquired. Congratulations Fiona! I am majorly proud of you and everybody here. We are all on the same side when it comes to making an enormous impact on the improvement of our environment, while we have a seriously good time. Well done."

234

At first it looked as if she did not understand what he said, but then burst into tears and threw her arms around Troy. One could hear a muffled "thank you, thank you" through the sound system as she nestled her head against his chest. In true style she regained her composure, held her fist high in the air and shouted at the crowd "thank you, you made it all worthwhile. Have a fantastic time!" High above her, the laser lights painted the word 'Indulge' against the clouds.

I was speechless. Every single person in that square stood up and cheered. Despite all her idiosyncrasies, she truly made a difference and I was very happy that I could be a participant.

"Before I introduce Matthew to you," Troy spoke into the microphone again, "let me just remind you that you and I are all committed to keep this place as clean as you found it. Please, we rely on you to be very strict with regard to the MOOP policy which you agreed upon when you booked your visit. MOOP means 'Matter out of Place'. It basically means that none of us will leave rubbish behind – not a cigarette butt or a bottle or anything – you take your own crap away. Unless you want to come here next time and party in a shithole. We are asking for your respect."

Again, the crowd responded with overwhelming approval.

"Ok, with that out of the way, here is Matthew. He is the one who organised your entertainment for the evening."

Matthew walked forward. He made quite an impression, in an understated self-assured way that made the crowd pay attention. After all, he looked the part; long blond dreads, a dark oversized vest, knee length shorts with skater shoes, muscled arms and legs covered in snake patterns.

"Yo!" he shouted and bowed. "I don't have much to say, accept that I hope you support Viper Beers. We are a bunch of piss cats, but we have good hearts. Have fun boys and girls! Big love. Peace." He held his fist in the air. The crowd responded again with cheers, whistles and fists.

Behind him the band completed their preparations for the final act. They gave Matthew the thumbs up.

"Here you go! Please show them how much you love them! Here is Goldfish!" With that he ran off stage.

All the lasers came on at once and the band kicked off, very appropriately, with 'One Million Views'. It was more or less the visitor count we had on our web pages. I grabbed myself a Premium and joined the crowd on the dancefloor. It was a really good evening and I was happy that it worked out well for all of us. We all had a reason why we needed it to work out well and it came together magnificently. It was what we worked for, what we looked forward to and finally achieved. How bloody awesome?!

A while later Matthew found me. We took our shirts off and danced with all the smiling faces around us. Our 'tattoos' caused quite a stir. At first a few people thought we were scary, but after a while they settled down and touched us.

I did not even try to respond when people ruminated "Wow bro, that's rad! Where did you have that done? I want sick tats like those." I loved the music too much. It was not the right time to chat.

It was after midnight when Matthew said to me: "c'mon brother, its quiet time for just you and me," he said. "Let's go. I've had enough."

We grabbed a couple of six-packs, hopped in Matthew's truck and drove all the way to the cemetery at the crest of the hill. He parked in exactly the same spot where we talked through the night the first time we met. This time he was more prepared and came armed with an old carpet, a couple of blankets and two cushions. We wrapped ourselves warmly and lay there looking at the stars - the moon was nowhere to be seen – which were at their most cheerful and brightest. Below us was the chapel spire in bright green and opposite it the band stand with an incredible display of light that changed to the rhythm of the music. Every now and again, the lasers reached out to touch the stars.

237

"I wonder ..." I said.

"Yes?"

"I wonder if creatures on those stars will be able to see that we had a party here a hundred million years from now. That is, if they are a hundred million light years away from us."

"That is such a cool thought Max. I wonder if they will boogie to our music." We laughed. While still looking at the stars he said: "I can imagine, we go through so many styles of music so quickly, they would really have to fine tune their receivers to get to the good stuff. Like Trance lasted for about five to ten years in a hundred million years and House for about the same. Classical music lasted for a bit longer – like two or three hundred of those years."

"Do you think creatures like that would get us, I mean understand us? Or do you think they would also think we just made weird noises like whales and cats?"

"I dunno bro," he said, "We make a lot of noises for things that mean the same thing or more or less the same thing."

"True," I said and looked at him, "like love. We say the word, but we don't even know what it means. Yet we feel it. We say it as a word, in sentences, in poems, in songs, in images, in things we do and even in the way we live..."

"Yes bro, and we say it out of context and we use it when we mean other things or when we just want to show our approval. For example, I loved spending the evening down there and I loved listening to the music, but I'm not in love with any of that."

We sat there staring at the sky. In the end Matthew broke the silence.

"Well, those aliens up there, will, a hundred million light years from now, be able to tune their tools and report to the Universal Bank of Intelligence that they discovered the most fucked-up creatures that ever lived and died - not soon enough because they also fucked up everything they touched because they tried to make things into things they were not."

"What do you mean?" I asked.

"For one, we try to convert everything into money. Did you see someone the other day patented the position they discovered for the location of a faulty gene that causes women to get breast cancer?"

"No."

"Some materialistic money hungry sick scientist is now going to make money out of that bit of knowledge. People are so fucked. They will do anything and everything to take from others to make their own pathetic lives better. I don't think the universe wanted us to compete with each other. We were supposed to

239

help each other and take care of each other, not destroy each other in an effort to get to the top of the pile."

"May I ask you a question Matt?"

"Yes, shoot. I hope I can answer your question," he said.

"What is going to happen to us? I mean you and I, we are different ..."

"Nothing," he said and laughed at me. "It's all going to be the same."

"What do you mean?"

"It's easy my brother. We are the lucky ones. Every one of those assholes down there will, at some or time, experience something that will change their lives – like in 'forever'. Some of them will notice it and some will talk it away and some will pretend it never happened. We cannot do that, because we are part of a consciousness that is so honest that it will always show. We can no longer hide behind lies and pretence."

"I like what you are saying, but I am still not sure I understand – I can see myself change in the mirror and in a strange way, I really like what is happening to me," I said.

"That is so cool, my brother! Some people do not and will never understand. One of the reasons you are cool with what is happening to you is because you also respect the change. If you did not, the change would have destroyed you."

"Now you have lost me," I said and stared at him.

"Do you remember, when we first went into that fridge, there was a boy next to that stupid Candy?"

"Yes, I always wanted to ask you about him because it looked as if he had a bite mark in his neck."

Matthew rolled on his side and looked at me seriously. "You remember how I said to you that this place gave me perspective? Well, I learnt that whatever is given to you should be respected. That kid broke into the distillery after a guest trip and drank himself into a coma on Premiums. He had no idea what he was doing and did not respect the juice he stole. Nobody knows what exactly happened, but we think he went there on a dare and after getting drunk he went into the snake pit. He got bitten in the neck. Strangely enough, he died before he could shed his skin, but most of the snakes still bonded with him. In the morning when he was found, all the snakes in that pit were wrapped around him as if they wanted to protect him, like they do with eggs."

"Hectic!"

"Hahahaha! Yes, bro, but you and I have gone through our transformation. That's why your first shed was so painful. We never have to come out to others about anything again. Those people down there are still hiding

241

behind their lies and pretence, regardless if they are gay or have a disease or if they are carrying the burden of some hectic guilt that their religion or parents had given them to carry as baggage for all their lives. You and I are free. We are just what we are. We cannot hide, because our journey is painted on our skin and in our eyes and it is incredibly beautiful."

"That is amazing Matt. Thank you. That is so cool. I get it. No more pretence, no more façade and none of the hard work that goes with that. I guess in future we will just mind our own business, bask in the sun and look out for each other until someone messes with us, but then they will see our nasty sides." I laughed and curled up next to him.

"We are lucky my friend, you will see the future and the past will become much less important – it is much better and a hell of a lot of fun to enjoy what is happening right now – without hang-ups and labels."

"I need to piss," I said and got up. "Me too," he said.

We walked a little distance from the graves, in respect for the dead, I guess, and took a leak while the party was going strong – complete with lights, lasers and more than just a hint of weed drifting across the valley – to the tune of "Choose your own Adventure."

I loved that band.

242

Chapter 11

A Brand-New Day

I was woken by voices in the street. Even though I did not get much sleep, I was curious about what was going on outside. A quick glance at my phone told me that it was just after eight in the morning. I flipped the bed sheets over to get up and instantly realised that Matthew's prediction about my shedding was correct. My skin was pale and dull and, to say the least, a little weird to touch.

The new shower was a joy even though I only spent a few minutes preparing myself for the day. Well that's what I thought. Nothing could have prepared me for the ruckus on the square that morning. Oblivious of the carnage at the factory the previous night, I dressed in casual shorts, a black t-shirt and a generous helping of Givenchy Play before I hit the streets. When I reached the main road, the aroma of fresh coffee and waffles made me walk straight to Minnie's without thinking. I craved breakfast and so did a few other half dead people who precariously surfaced, or who were still awake after an all-night bender. I could see from far away that Minnie's place was packed.

The noise came from a group of people that stood next to the white TV van parked opposite the deli. Oh no, I thought, not them again. Everybody had so much fun and in contrast that television woman was such a damper on everything. She and her cameraman were completely uninvited and somehow managed to get past the entrance gate despite Troy's specific instructions that only people with valid entry tickets should be allowed to get in. There was no doubt in my mind that they fabricated some story and the boys believed them.

It turned out that when Troy went to check up on Claws production in the morning, he noticed the TV vehicle in the parking area. When he looked around, he could not find Christina or the cameraman. He then called Minnie and asked if she had seen them. As it happened, Candy and the cameraman were having breakfast. She looked as if he had made love to her relentlessly and ardently to the point that she was barely capable of coping with any posture other than lying down. She sat quietly in her chair sucking, this time, on a thick straw which she held gingerly between her thumb and index fingers in a glass of ginger and carrot juice. He, on the other hand, had a beer in his hand and sported the biggest grin imaginable on his face, a look only achievable in a state of afterglow or bliss, whichever you prefer.

"Excuse me," Minnie interrupted them, "your vehicle was found at the lion food production facility at Cheerio. The keys were still in the ignition, but nobody can find your colleague. Do you by any chance know anything about her whereabouts?"

"No, I gave her the vehicle – I don't know – between nine and ten last night. I have not seen her since."

"Everybody at the factory was concerned. You know, you should never leave keys and valuables in a vehicle. Things get stolen in no time. I'm just pleased on your behalf that nothing bad has happened," Minnie said and returned to the kitchen to check on a fresh batch of waffles.

"What was that all about?" Candy wanted to know, in a rather subdued, crackly voice after her heavy night. She stuck her fingers in her hair in an attempt to shape the dishevelled arrangement on her head and scratched her scalp at the same time.

"My colleague, Christina, was following up on some story she wanted to report on. I don't quite know. She left before I saw you."

Candy was enchanted. He had a gorgeous Irish brogue which was entirely new to her and she found it completely irresistible. Every time he opened his mouth, she just wanted to kiss him, never mind listening to what he had to say. She gawked at him and combed the knots out of her hair with her fingers.

The silence was broken when the TV van roared up the road towards the deli and came to a standstill in the parking area across the road.

"Oh, there she is now babe. I wonder what the hell she did last night."

"What is your name again?" Candy asked and giggled.

"Don't tell me you cannot remember Cindy; my name is Mackey. I bet that's the only part of me that was forgettable. Hahahaha!"

"Candy," she said and put her virgin face on.

"Oh I'm sorry, I meant Candy." He looked at her, just a tad embarrassed and noticed how his two-day old stubble left glow spots all over her mouth, cheeks and chin. The poor girl was going to have scabs on her face and stretch marks everywhere else, he thought proudly.

It was not Christina who got out of the vehicle, but Troy. He power walked across the street to the restaurant.

"Hey brother, is this your truck, hey?"

"Yes, it is."

"Why was it at the factory, hey? Minnie said that woman who was with you left it there. What the fuck was she doing there, last night, while we were having a party?" Troy was, for good reason, irritated and he made no attempt to hide it.

Mackey quickly came out of his afterglow and found himself on the defensive.

"I'm sorry man, I don't know. After she had a fight with that Fiona woman last night, she decided to follow the old man with the black SUV. She wanted to see what he was up to. I never saw her again after that."

"Here are your keys. I asked the workers at the factory to look for her – it is very strange that she just disappeared. Where are you staying over?"

"At the hotel in the forest." Mackey got up from the table. He was a big man, despite his young age, with a light olive skin tone that loved covering his balding head with a tweed cap. "Look, there is no need to be aggressive with me. I don't know what happened. Thanks for the keys."

"Look here bro, fuck you and that fucking woman you came here with. Something tells me that you are being dishonest and I promise you - I'll fuck you up good and solid. We have a fucking festival going on here and now this fuckup. You are not welcome here, so I suggest you take your van and get the fuck out of here! How did you get in here anyway?"

"Look, I don't know your name …"

"Troy bro, my fucking name is Troy and remember my name because I'm gonna come after you and break your fucking knees if I find out that you did not tell me the truth."

"Look ... Troy, I'm really sorry, I don't want to cause any trouble. Everybody, especially Cindy, u'hum, Candy have been really nice to me. I had a great party with everybody and I want to stay for the big one tonight. Christina was on her own mission."

"What the fuck was her mission brother? If I know I might just find the bitch quicker so that we can get going with our arrangements for tonight."

It was more or less at that time I arrived at the restaurant. By then Troy was not holding back. Mackey, on the other hand, remained calm and unfazed.

"She wanted to find out if there was anything untoward happening here which she could use as a television report. That's how we make a living. If we have dull stories that are not aired, we don't get paid. That's why she was so determined. She said that she was going to follow the old man. That's all. She was working on a hunch. I promise you, between friends, that's all I know. Maybe she went home with the old man."

Now that was a morbid thought.

"I'm not your fucking friend bro! I don't even know you. I cannot imagine that anybody, but the dead, would want to go home with Desfourneaux. But I'll find out."

"Can I make a suggestion Troy," I interrupted, "perhaps we should get the search and rescue people involved.

They are much better equipped than anybody else to find someone who is lost. Would you like me to call them?"

"Yes, brother that's a great idea. Call them because I don't fucking know what to do and I have to help Matthew with the line-up this evening."

I fortunately had the number of the lady who was in charge of Search and Rescue's number on my phone. We once went on a hike and when we reached the highest point amongst the surrounding mountains, she produced a cheese platter and champagne out of nowhere for us to enjoy. Her name was Odette. She was super cool and told me that she grew up in the mountains, where they always played and fooled around as kids. She, without a doubt, knew the area better than anybody else and successfully rescued countless people from the mountain, the river and even at the base of one of the waterfalls. More recently, Fiona had her trained to deal with the lions just in case some nutcase went into the paddocks at Panthera Park.

Odette arrived with Lieutenant Lourens from the Police Service. While they had discussions with Troy and Mackey, I went into the kitchen for a chat with Minnie. She was exhausted, but could not hide her excitement.

"I am so grateful," she said, "I have made enough money in the past two days to get rid of my overdraft. It is such a relief. Thank you, Max, for your help with the new menu. It is very popular with everybody."

"It's a pleasure. And great, it was fun, but I think we need to add a few more vegan meals. Many of the hippies out there are vegan."

"You are right Max, quite a few of them asked, but I was prepared." She grinned at me sneakily and said: "You taught me well, so I looked on the Internet for vegan waffle recipes and modified my basic recipe. They turned out fantastically and everybody loved them."

"Well done!"

"And ... I made my own almond and cashew nut butter too!" She giggled, stuck her finger in a container, scooped out some of the contents and put it in my mouth. "Now tell me that is not the best almond butter you have ever tasted!"

"Mmmmmm," was the only sound I could produce. It was sensational – smooth, but not too creamy and certainly not oily; an underlying nuttiness with just a tiny hint of bitterness that was unmistakeably the taste of natural almonds grown in the vicinity - pure heaven.

While I was sampling the new delights that Minnie concocted, Lieutenant Lourens took control of the situation outside. He was also a local boy that grew up on a farm not far from Cheerio. Herding cattle, horse riding and swimming in the river shaped him into a human specimen that even Leonardo da Vinci would have drooled over. Towards the end of his teens he was also blessed with an abundance of testosterone, which presumably fired up his pheromones to such a degree that whoever was in his company instantly forgot their parental warnings about extramarital intimacy. As a result, throughout his school years, he received considerable attention from the girls, and a few boys, who craved his company for, shall we say, Darwinian reasons and not for scholarly purposes. Everybody knew that Lourens was well-endowed but not well-informed. His natural instincts allowed him to embrace the opportunities that were liberally offered to him and consequently his physical abilities were often the topic of hushed nocturnal conversations.

Needless to say that Lourens's touch made him well loved in the village. After he came back from the police training college, he was better looking than ever in his uniform and sported a new tattoo that one could see hiding under the right sleeve of his shirt. Once, when he walked across the road towards the Police Station from her restaurant, Minnie was shocked to hear one of her patrons say that his ass cheeks were so tight they could crack a nut. When she looked over her reading glasses, she secretly had to admit that there was nothing wrong with the client's observation.

At the Police Training College, Lourens acquired various techniques that added professionalism to his approach. He came back with numerous 'To Do' lists which his companions at the college helped him compile. These lists ranged from 'To Do List for a Car Theft' to 'To Do List for Drunk Driving'. He fortunately had a 'To Do List for a Missing Person', which he brought with him to the restaurant. He carefully went through the questionnaire with Mackey and established that he was the last person who spent time with Christina. He noted word for word what Mackey said about her departure and the GoPro camera. Candy corroborated Mackey's statement that he spent the night at the festival in her presence. Lourens had one look at her and concluded that he was not only in her presence, but also in her panties. After all, one professional can easily spot another's good work.

"Thank you Mackey," he said. "Troy, who was on duty at the gate last night?"

"I'm not sure brother, but I will find out for you and make sure you can talk to the boys."

"Thank you. Please will you fetch Mr Desfourneaux so that I can talk to him too?"

"Sure brother. No problem. I'll fetch him."

Lourens excused himself and walked to the entrance gate. Everyone could see how he talked to the lumberjack boys and scribbled on his note pad. Odette left to arrange a search party and Troy walked in the opposite direction to fetch the old man. Suddenly, I was alone with Mackey and Candy. We looked at one another awkwardly.

"Whaaaaa! You are the one with the awesome tattoos! Mackey, you should see he and his brother have the same tattoos! It is so rad to see the two of them together."

"Ahhh, its nothing." I said and blushed, thinking what Mackey was probably thinking.

"They are really cool. They do everything together." Candy carried on. "I got very drunk with them one evening. We had lots of fun."

"What happened to you that evening? We searched for you."

"I had the worst case of the munchies ever. I remembered that I had chocolates in my car, and went to fetch it but the rain came down and I fell asleep in the car. Thanks for a really sick evening."

She was nicer than I thought. "Yeah, I had a great evening too. But we were worried."

"Never mind," she said, "let's have as much fun as possible this weekend. I loved Goldfish. Who is the headline band tonight?"

"I have no idea," I replied, "Matthew arranged the entertainment. We will have to ask him."

"Ok, let's have a Tequila to get this day going properly." Mackey surprised me and who was I to decline?

When Minnie looked in our direction I waved her over. "Please can we have four tequilas? One is for you."

"Of course my darling," she said and a minute later returned with a bottle and four tot glasses.

"On a brilliant night tonight," she said as she poured the drinks.

"Yeah!" we chorused and downed the liquid.

Troy arrived with Desfourneaux a few minutes later. He looked cheerful and relaxed despite his usual miserable attire. Troy, on the other hand, was tight lipped and distant. Since I got to know him, I learnt that Troy was extremely disciplined. His meticulous nature made him a slave of predictability. If anything was in the way of his expectation, he became grumpy and difficult. If his plans worked out well, then he was invariably in a jovial mood, punctuated by infectious laughs and surprising acts of random kindness. We all knew that he basically ran Fiona's farm. Yes, she was the big talker with the thick wallet, but it was Troy who made it happen. And because he made it happen, he did not take shit from anybody. One of the qualities I really liked about him was his earthy, basic philosophy about subjects most academics would write endless volumes. On the first day he met me, he said to me: "Brother I don't care who you fuck or who fucks you. If you are a good person, I'll be your friend." I was taken aback and laughed like a retard, not knowing what to say, but I bonded with him right there and then.

His no-nonsense outlook on life coupled with his stocky swimmer's build made him a formidable opponent, which I think, he could take to a physical level quite easily. He told me that he was a "wild fucker" when he was young, that he did cage fighting for fun and that he would break people's knees for his friends. I liked his level of commitment but steered clear of the violence. Just as well that he was a teetotaller. I did not want to be on his wrong side if he was inebriated. That particular Saturday was one of the days he should have stayed at home.

By the time Lourens returned, Minnie had breakfast ready for all of us – poached eggs, trout fillets, served on small triangular waffles; dressed with Hollandaise Sauce and a little side salad.

Lourens started the conversation bluntly: "Mr Desfourneaux, please could you tell me what you did last night?"

Desfourneaux turned white. "U'hum, I was around here at the festival, but it was too noisy for me, so I went home."

"Are you sure about that?" Lourens inquired from him, "Because the people at the gate told me that you left and came back two hours later. Where did you go at the middle of the night?"

"That is none of your business. I'm a free man and I can do whatever I like!"

"Does that mean you left the village for a few hours late last night?" Lourens held his pen firmly and waited for the old man.

"Yes," Desfourneaux replied.

Lourens finished the last of his coffee. "Mr Desfourneaux, you must please be honest with me. This is a very serious issue and I intend to get to the bottom of it. Your demeanour tells me that you are hiding something. Perhaps you should come with me to the police station for a formal interview. Thank you for the breakfast Minnie. Please add the meal to my tab. I'll sort you out later. Mr Desfourneaux, please come with me."

The old man started to shake.

"I'll tell you everything, just please don't take me there. I don't belong in jail. I did it because I had no alternative. *Oh, mon cher Dieu pardonne-moi!* I did it because the crematorium had blown up!"

He cracked like a Tennis Biscuit. Nobody said a word. Lourens shook his head. "What does the crematorium have to do with this? I just asked where you went last night. What did you do?"

"I put them in the machine," Desfourneaux shouted.

"What? What are you talking about? What did you put in the machine?"

"I put Mary Rose and the dog in the machine because the crematorium didn't work and I did not have an alternative."

Lourens looked up from his notes and stared at Desfourneaux. "Mr Desfourneaux. Go slowly now. What does that have to do with Christina?"

"Who is Christina?" Desfourneaux replied.

"The television presenter woman," Troy responded.

"What about her? I don't know her. I saw her in the chapel when she upset Fiona. She was with him," and pointed at Mackey.

"That's true," said Mackey. "But we believe that she followed you last night, sir. We cannot find her."

"I never saw her." Desfourneaux realised that he should have kept quiet and bowed his head.

"Are you sure about that?" Lourens persisted.

"I never saw her last night. The only time I ever saw her was in the chapel."

"Well Mr Desfourneaux," Lourens continued, "we have it on record that she followed you last night. Where did you go?"

"I went to Cheerio."

"Why?"

We all kept quiet while Lourens tried to extract the truth from Desfourneaux. Minnie, in the meantime, offered more coffee which we all accepted. We all knew that Desfourneaux was weird but it was unlikely that he would have caused physical harm to anybody else. He was much too frail for that.

Lourens repeated: "Why, Mr Desfourneaux, did you go to Cheerio last night?"

Desfourneaux just stared at the floor. He knew that he was in trouble.

"Why Mr Desfourneaux? I don't have time. We have to find that lady."

"I went to my farm. I told you."

"Did you see Christina at the farm Mr Desfourneaux?"

"No, I did not. I went into the machine room and the freezer. That's all. I never saw that woman. Why would she follow me anyway? That is stupid."

Lourens was satisfied that he got enough out of Desfourneaux and warned him. "Mr Desfourneaux, we are going to search for Christina. In the mean-time you are not allowed to leave the area without my knowledge. You are a person of interest in the disappearance of this lady."

Without a further word, Lourens got up and walked across the road to the police station. Minnie looked at him, rolled a walnut in her palms and squeezed it hard. At his office, Lourens called his divisional superiors and asked for assistance. A little later search teams arrived from the surrounding towns.

I walked up the road to Fiona's shop with Troy.

"I'm not in a good space brother," he said. "There is something about this thing that is messing with my head."

"How so?"

"Since I was young, I was somewhat psychic, I would say. Please don't talk to anybody about this. People will think I am peculiar, but seriously brother, I believe in the supernatural. There is something that is making me upset and I have a feeling that my bones are being broken."

"Oh come on Troy," I said "things will be ok. Don't stress so much about everything."

"Look brother, everybody in this village risked their last penny on the success of this festival. If it is a mess, we will all be ruined. We need this to get this village to function properly again. We cannot afford something bad to happen. But somehow, I cannot help it, when I got into that TV van, I got a feeling that I was being crushed from my head down to my feet. Like … when … if one of those road compacting rollers went over me."

"Damn, that's hectic Troy."

"You know, I once had a dream that I went to a restaurant with my girlfriend at the time. In the dream I could see the inside of the place and that it faced a cobblestone road. I told my girlfriend and as true as god that night when we went out, we went to a place that was exactly as the place in my dream with the cobblestone road."

"Wow! That's amazing!"

"At first it scared me, but now I know these feelings are good for me. They sometimes warn me about bad things and I have a bad feeling about this woman."

"Let's stay positive…"

"Brother, there is shit written all over this fucking story. Something really bad happened to that woman and it is no good. She worked for a television company. When news gets out that shit happened here, it will be all over the news all over the world. She will end up being her own fucking story."

"That will be after the festival Troy. C'mon, let's make the best of the last day. Tomorrow everyone will go back home with, hopefully, lots of new numbers and Facebook friends."

"You are right brother. Let's do it."

Fiona had tea with Matthew when we arrived at her shop.

"Good morning boys!" she said. "Your timing is perfect. We just made a fresh pot of tea."

"Thanks, but we had coffee down the road a minute ago," I replied.

"Not for me either," Troy said and waved his hand.

"Never mind, I have delicious biscuits …"

"Howzit Matt." I was pleased to see him and grinned, then looked at Fiona and asked: "What did the two of you get up to last night? Incidentally, you looked absolutely stunning on stage last night. Congratulations!"

"Oh, we had a wonderful time. We danced until everyone got legless and then I dropped Troy off at the gate so that he could reconcile with the boys that manned the entrance."

"Yes brother, you know I don't drink, so when the people get too drunk, they just irritate me."

Matthew checked them out and winked at me. "I saw you left early," he said. "It was such a good party, I wondered why."

Troy and Fiona looked at each other and blushed.

"So what did you get up to?" Fiona looked in my direction.

Before I could say a thing, Matthew explained that we went to the cemetery to do star gazing and to look at the party down in the valley.

"It was awesome. We had to cuddle up to each other because it was damn cold, but it was so awesome, I'll remember it for a long time. It was a truly special occasion," he said.

"Now that is one place you will not get me at night," Troy said. "There are two things I am terrified of, snakes and ghosts. I once went to that cemetery at sun set and there was such weird energy, I could not stand it. I almost broke my truck's left front wheel, I drove down that hill so fast.

"I think it sounds lovely," Fiona said, "but what's the story with the woman from the TV station?"

"Oh, fuck, don't even remind me of that," Troy replied, "Apparently she went to Cheerio to spy on Desfourneaux of all people, and then disappeared. The search and rescue people are looking for her."

264

"You know she went into our snake pit the previous night?" Matthew said, "That woman is seriously irresponsible and probably got herself into trouble again. The silly bitch!"

While we were talking, a police vehicle drove up the road and parked at Desfourneaux's house. Lourens got out. A little later we saw a handcuffed Desfourneaux being ushered into the back of the car.

"What the fuck ..." came out of Troy's mouth, but it echoed what we all thought.

"No! There must be a mistake ... I'm going to find out what the hell is going on," Matthew said and ran across the road. By the time he reached the police vehicle he could hear Lourens saying to a sobbing Desfourneaux: "I am taking you into custody as a person of interest on suspicion of the murder of Christina Amperboer as well as that you unlawfully and intentionally violated a corpse."

"Lourens, bro, you are making a big mistake. How could this man possibly have murdered a healthy woman? Look at him – he is halfway between leather and dust! Even if he wanted to, it would have been like an ant trying to kill an elephant. For heaven's sake, he cannot even keep up with a motorised lawn mower. Have you lost your mind?" Matthew stood between Lourens and the car with his back to Desfourneaux. "Seriously bro, you are making a big mistake."

"Get out of my way Matthew. I'm doing my job," Lourens said and walked around him to the close the passenger door. "The search and rescue team found the woman's high heel shoes in the building at Cheerio. It is highly unlikely that she would have walked anywhere without shoes. There were only two people in that building. One is alive and one is missing. I intend to find out what happened to her. You can tell Troy for me that all production at the factory must be stopped until the forensic people have taken samples everywhere."

Lourens got in the car and drove to the police station.

"He is fucking bonkers, that stupid policeman," Troy said when Matthew got back. "What are they going to do? The production team put a whole dead giraffe through that machine this morning and now he wants to do forensics? A giraffe bro. A whole fucking giraffe. Whatever evidence there was, will be contaminated by now. The thought of Desfourneaux killing someone is beyond ridiculous. If that stupid Lourens was in stature as low as he was in intellect, he could kiss the ass of a rat without bending his knees!"

"Guys, let's focus," I said. "We have a big night ahead of us. Let's make this one even more awesome than the night before. What do you think Fiona? You have been unbelievably quiet."

"I did not mean to be quiet, but I just wondered if we should make a statement about the woman's disappearance?"

"If I were you, I would not say a word," I replied. "Remember everyone in this village saw you had a drama with that woman last night – and you left early. Lourens might just come to the conclusion that you and Troy had something to do with her disappearance."

"Are you out of your fucking mind?" Troy was not having any of that.

"No Troy, I'm merely trying to think like Lourens. He will have to follow up on every lead unless Desfourneaux is found to be guilty as sin, but there are no witnesses. Frankly Matthew and I have no alibi either. We cannot call the stars as witnesses …"

"Shit! This is getting worse by the minute. Troy, please give me my bag!" When Troy gave Fiona her bag, she, as usual, found the box of Urbanol without looking and dislodged a pill without taking her eyes off me. "Don't say that Max! That woman accused me of being the queen of a grasping and mendacious hierarchy of greed. Of course I had to get rid of her, and I am sure I was not the first who had harsh words with her. I acted in self-defence."

"No Fiona! Damn, you cannot say that! If you say that you got rid of her and acted in self-defence, it sounds as if you killed her. Be a little more careful with your choice of words!" Fiona exasperated me sometimes. "Be careful to just state the facts – no feelings. Unless you did have something to do with her disappearance?"

"Fuck you brother! Don't go there. Fiona was with me." Troy shouted at me.

"Well you don't have to prove it to me, but if Lourens asks, then you better be sure of yourself and be honest. I believe you were together." I winked at the two of them. Matthew did not let them get away that easily. "Oh yes, you two naughty bums! I always thought there was something going on between the two of you. Cute! I love it, you have my blessing."

"Not so fast Matthew," Fiona interrupted. "What he meant was that I was with him at the time when Desfourneaux was at Cheerio. We certainly did not spend the night together. We danced and had alcohol free champagne and canapés at the waterfall while the party was still going strong. Troy had to check that the shift-change at the gate went smoothly."

"Ok, enough about last night. Let's get out of here and get organised," Matthew abruptly ended the conversation. "I have a massive surprise waiting for all of you." I agreed to meet him at the beer stall and we said our goodbyes.

"Cheers Fiona. See you soon." Troy and I walked back to the square. It was lunchtime. There was a delicious smell of boerewors rolls and beer in the air. The first DJ was stirring up the crowd with some gentle, laidback trance. Down in the valley, one could hear police vehicle sirens rush in the direction of Cheerio.

When we reached the road, Troy started to laugh all by himself. "Tonight is the last night of our party. So are you going to get laid tonight brother?"

"I should hope so," I laughed back at him. "I'd love some naughty fun tonight."

"Are you sorted? Do you need some assistance?"

"I'm not sure what you mean Troy."

"I have some pills to make you extra strong."

"Seriously?" I laughed out loudly. "Well I guess one can never be too sure!"

He fumbled in his pocket and gave me a blister pack with four odd shaped pills. "Those are 100mg brother. You break them in two and take only half. If you take a whole one, it will blow your head off. They are fucking awesome. If you take a half, there are enough for eight good fucks in there. Fiona loves it when I take them. She said that I fuck like a porn star."

Troy stopped, took a deep breath and said in a hushed voice, as if there was anybody that could hear: "Shit, I wasn't supposed to say that. She is still secretive about us getting it together. Please don't say anything."

"Sure brother. I'll leave it up to you to say, what you need to say, whenever you are ready."

We laughed and put our fists together.

Fiona had a toy boy, I thought. Good for her!

The afternoon was quite chilled. I took a group of visitors to the waterfalls; Matthew took a slightly more daring bunch to check out the brewery; Troy took a few insanely noisy crazies to go zip-lining and Fiona took the largest group to Panthera Park. We agreed to get back at sunset, which was around six that afternoon, for the start of the evening fun.

When I walked back to my cottage to have a shower, I saw Desfourneaux outside the Spit and Polish. He looked even more exhausted than normal. He was also drunk as a skunk. "What's happening?" I asked.

"They let me go. Lieutenant Lourens and the forensic people were all over me since this morning. They gave me a lie detector test and then let me go. But they charged me for making lion food out of Mary Rose."

"Are you ok?"

"No. My life is ruined Max. My chickens died, my crematorium exploded, my cash ran out when Fiona took charge of my farm, I had problems with Mary Rose and now this. I don't think I can handle things any longer. I'm supposed to be a professional, but I am no longer in control."

"I think you should get some rest. We are going to have great fun tonight."

I took him by the hand and walked with him to his house. It was the first time I went there. Suffice to say that it was austere and forbidding, but spotlessly clean. I led Desfourneaux into the sitting room, which was furnished with Imbuia ball-and-claw furniture, a carpet with wild orange patterns, similar to one my aunt had many years ago and curtains with brownish floral outline patterns that ended halfway between the windowsill and the floor. A plastic flower arrangement, presumably made for a coffin, attempted to cheer up the coffee table which was covered with a white lace table cloth.

I looked around. There were small pictures in thin black frames against large blank walls that somehow resonated with the dark wood architraves around all the doors. The place was not just austere but also depressing – perhaps because it reminded me of my grandmother's house on the farm. All the beautiful features, such as the incredible stone walls and massive beams that stretched across the roof of the sitting room, were diminished by the beige walls and the dreadful furnishings.

When the old man sat down, I was overcome with sadness. The image of him, in his black suit and infernal

271

black tie, sitting on that hideous brown couch, was the quintessence of an abandoned old person who desperately tried to remain relevant and independent. Behind that curmudgeonly abrasiveness was a sweet soul he could not hide. He looked so frail and defeated that I forgot about, what appeared to me, his slimy behaviour and insatiable scheming to make another buck. Perhaps his way of making a living just lacked the marketing gloss of Fiona's efforts? It was all the same, there was just a lack of class and sophistication. But who was I to judge? I did not understand the challenges of old age and, especially, his solitude.

"Can I make you some tea?" I asked, but he did not respond. He was fast asleep.

Before I left, I took a pillow and blanket off his bed which I used to make him a little more comfortable.

When I was done, I whispered, "Rest well my friend. Tomorrow will bring a better day. I know you only did the best you could under the circumstances. If you feel like it later, come and have a boogie with us."

He briefly opened his eyes before I closed the door behind me.

At eight that evening the party was in full swing under a cloudless sky. There was a cross section of all ages and genders and colours on the dance floor making the event their own. But there was also a collective energy that created cohesion amongst all of us. Surprisingly, I felt very much at home with the visitors. With the exception of the dreaded Christina, there was a sense of joyful anticipation amongst them that bubbled into laughter, camaraderie and fun. Life was supposed to be about fun and discovery despite the undercurrents of evil, deceit and dishonesty. Somehow, the mask of pretence was also stripped off the faces of the people I got to know in the village. They revealed a level of authenticity and truthfulness about themselves that was intoxicating. This shift in my reality made me wonder if I was perhaps experiencing a changing ability to not only see, but also to perceive. Was I starting to grasp things differently? Was I starting to learn to look past the bullshit and see humans as if they were infrared images? These thoughts were scary, but pretty beguiling at the same time.

By the time I arrived at my beer station, the village was awash with a different set of secret lights that were not revealed the previous evening. To my surprise even the trees that lined the border of the rain forest had little lights that stepped all the way to the stars. Below them, the hammocks were illuminated with UV lights that gave them completely different colours. The lights from the road were adjusted to twinkle with the ones in the trees. Unlike the previous evening, all the lights were pure white.

273

At exactly eight thirty, a thundering noise approached from the south. When I looked up, Matthew stood in front of me with his right hand in the air.

"Surprise!" He said and gave me his lapdog smile with his tongue hanging out.

I responded with a high five across the beer counter.

"What is happening?"

"I know you are going to love this," he said and smiled a smile so broad I thought his lips would crack. He could not look at me. His eyes searched for the horizon and then stepped up a little towards the clouds and then back to the horizon again. He smiled with such delight that little tears formed in the corners of his eyes. It was the first time that I ever saw him like that. He looked as if he loved the moment so much that he was tickled on the inside, squirming with joy. What could I do? I just laughed at him.

I tried to talk to Matthew, but the roar in the sky became so loud that it was impossible to communicate at all. Suddenly it became brightly illuminated, that made it look like a space ship. It was a helicopter with all its lights switched on at the same time.

"Wait for it!" Matthew shouted at me and ran to the stage. I could see him going up the steps along the side and across the stage. At the centre, he stopped, grinned at the audience and then screamed into the microphone:

274

"Get ready everybody! If you don't have a drink yet, you have about 20 seconds to get what you need. We have the biggest and best surprise for you!" Thundering music blasted through the speakers to welcome the helicopter while the crowd responded to Matthew with equally tumultuous applause. Hundreds of miniature copies of the event reflected on the back of cell phones in front of me.

As the spectacle unfolded, more visitors and locals appeared from everywhere – from the cottages, B&B's, pubs, restaurants, tents, hammocks and the forest. The greatest show the village had ever seen was about to start. At the last moment Lieutenant Lourens and Dr Riaan emerged from the Police Station. By then, the search for Christina was terminated because one of the forensic investigators found smudges of her lipstick on the feeder hopper. It was a huge stroke of luck after the giraffe went through the machine as well. Thankfully the MAC smudge resistant lipstick allowed them to conclude the search and rescue effort with a finding of accidental death pending a DNA confirmation.

The helicopter edged closer until it came to a halt above the band stand. Surprisingly, the wind generated by the propellers did not ruin the carnival decorations. From where I stood, I could see a rope ladder being lowered, followed by a figure. Troy ran like an athlete across the stage to secure the ladder. When he was done, he waved a thumbs up at the supporting crew. The signs were for the mobilisation of a crane to the side of the stage that unfolded with Mackey at the controls. At the end of the contraption was a video camera that made the gigantic screen behind Matthew come to life. Everybody could see the figure coming down on the rope ladder. When they recognised him, the crowd went mad.

"Tell him how glad you are to see him! Say welcome to ATB!"

Matthew hurled the words into the crowd. When the figure touched the stage, the plane took off and bombarded the village square with laser lights. All around the dancefloor were explosions in unison that released millions of bubbles over the crowd. It was magical.

"Now say hello to Sean Ryan," Matthew roared into the microphone. Another figure appeared from backstage. They exchanged a few words before Matthew walked to the edge of the stage, grabbed the microphone and said: "This is for you Max." He then handed the microphone to the guest and walked backwards to the steps before he disappeared into the crowd.

Seconds before the music started, Troy activated the set of main speakers and flooded the sky with a completely different arrangement of lights. The introductory beat echoed across the valley, massively, sumptuously, completely. Sean's smoky voice danced all over the rhythm, gave the beat meaning while he chewed, in his familiar fashion, on every word.

"Cold,
stay down,
don't say a word
I hear, I fear.

Deep,
life beats down beneath your skin,
beneath,
a world away.

On and on with every day.
We're alive and we're okay."

I was speechless. Here in the middle of nowhere was one of my favourite DJ's in the world playing some of my most favourite music. Music that I associated with an incredible array of good things. Nothing mattered anymore. I could not give a damn about the beer and the bullshit of the previous days that, frankly, had nothing to do with me. Below the counter were many Viper Premiums. While staring at the screen, I unscrewed a bottle and downed it. In the distance I could see Matthew waving at me. I grabbed a six pack and hooked up with him in the middle of the dancefloor.

"Wow!" I said and embraced him. "Thank you."

He just grinned at me and said: "Take off your clothes bro, I'm gonna shed!"

As if it was the most natural thing in the world, we took our shirts off, then our shoes, and danced to the more energetic rhythms, the band played for us, only in our shorts.

"Give me a drink!" he shouted.

I unscrewed two bottles and passed one on to him. We clinked the bottles and drank the Viper while feeling the rhythm in our feet.

And then it started – my vision became disturbed. Whatever I saw appeared to shake ever so slightly. My image of Matthew became somewhat smooth and perhaps even furry. I could see him throwing his head back; riding the ripples that ran down his spine into the curves of his ass. My convulsions started gently with little cramps around my belly; then with contractions up to the T-junction at my shoulders. Over and over; again and again. Rhythm and contractions blended into a delicious combination of earthiness and indulgence.

Far, far, far away
Out of body I will stay
Replace the memories
That I couldn't bring with me
The less that I can feel
The further I can go

The tear in my skin came as suddenly as before, from my forehead across my nose and splitting my upper lip in half. I gave myself to the music and what was happening to me without resistance, dancing to a primordial beat ingrained in my bones; superbly choreographed by a master musician who understood the cadence of life. Matthew's hand found mine and drew me closer to him. Our bodies touched, our energy became one and took me into a dream state. When I looked up at the stars, my body tore open from the centre of my chest, upwards through my Adam's apple and across my shoulders through the hinges of my elbows; along my forearms, through the palms of my hands and finally - the tips of my fingers.

I pealed the skin off my eyes. Without opening my eyes, I took Matthews hand and put it on my heart.

Far, far, far away
All my thoughts are lost at sea
Only half the sacrifice
Only half the life
Far, far, far away
This is where I came to stay

Around us, I could hear words fading in an out. "That is rad bro! Where did you get that morph suit? I want one too!"

"Have one of these," I said and pointed at my supercharged beers.

When I finally opened my eyes, Matthew was dancing with his back to me. He was covered in the most beautiful skin, radiant and glossy, with extraordinary patterns reaching from the contours of his ass to the undulated curves of his shoulders. The sheer power exuded from the depths of his patination made him look sculptural, a work of art.

It was time to crack one of those pills in half, I thought. With some effort, I removed the last skin from my hands and fumbled in my pocket. It was easy to unseat the tablet out of its home. I broke it in my palm and put one half in my mouth, then touched Matthew on the shoulder to let him have his half.

He turned round, but when he smiled his familiar lapdog smile, I noticed that he had new teeth and his tongue was deeply forked.

A power failure turned the festivities into pandemonium. Hundreds of phone torches quickly illuminated the space with modern candle light. Out of nowhere three figures appeared on the far side of the stage – an old, somewhat overweight woman in comfortable clothes and a middle-aged woman, smartly dressed, without shoes, walking a vicious looking dog on a leash. The luminescent diaphanous figures strolled gently across the podium. When they reached the centre, at the microphone stand, they briefly stopped, waved at the stunned audience and carried on walking to the other side. A gust of wind from the north scooped them up and transformed them into millions of claw shaped confetti that rained upon the crowd.

"Oh my fuck! Rose and Christina!" It was Troy's unmistakable voice. "Get me out of here! Get me fucking out of here!"

A stampede reverberated through the podium floorboards. As mysteriously as the power went out, it came back on. My eyes were still not functioning well, but I could see Troy running across the stage into the arms of Fiona, who was standing at the steps. She nervously prepared her thank you and closing speech, which she was supposed to deliver at the end of the final playlist. It never happened.

"Calm down honey! You are safe with me. Let me give you a tranquillizer."

She fumbled in her Matewis Maree hand stitched shoulder bag with her left hand, while wiping the sweat off his forehead with her other hand. She freed the pill, as usual, without looking and put it in his mouth. He gulped it down and begged her to take him home. The two of them left the square amongst huge audience applause and drove away in the silver Land Rover.

Unbeknownst to her, this time, in her haste, her hand found a different blister pack. Troy's head was blown off a little later.

281

More or less, at that time, the lions at Panthera Park woke up to a female voice from the manor house. Fortunately, the sounds had nothing to do with nightmares. They roared in approval and had another mouthful of giraffe flavoured Claws as a late night snack.

On the other side of the hill, the party ran its course. Energetic moves gave way to cuddle puddles and chats that stretched into the early morning, accompanied by chilled music with lyrics about the stars. Bonds were formed and others broken.

It was another bookmark in our journey.